LOWRY'S REVENGE

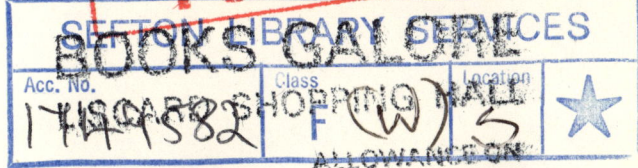
RON WATKINS

A Black Horse Western

ROBERT HALE · LONDON

Photoset in North Wales by
Derek Doyle & Associates, Mold, Clwyd.
Printed and bound in Great Britain by
WBC Book Manufacturers Limited,
Bridgend, Mid-Glamorgan.

For Gary and Penny

ONE

' "Howl, howl, howl, howl! O, you are men of
  stones!
Had I your tongues and eyes, I'd use them so
That heaven's vault should crack. She's gone
  for ever.
I know when one is dead and when one lives:
She's dead as earth. Lend me a looking-glass;
If that her breath will mist or stain the stone,
Why then she lives." '

The silent audience watched, spellbound, as
King Lear, holding the dead Cordelia in his arms,
tried to see whether there was any sign of life.
There was none.

There was the sound of a commotion outside the
hall.

' "A plague upon you, murderers, traitors all!
I might have saved her; now she's gone for
  ever.

7

Cordelia! Cordelia! stay a little." '

Several cowboys burst into the back of the hall. The actor ignored them.

> ' "What is it thou say'st? Her voice was ever soft,
> Gentle and low – an excellent thing in woman." '

One of the cowboys drew his pistol. He fired it into the air. 'That'll wake her up.' He slurred his words. He was obviously drunk.

His half-dozen or so companions laughed. The two actors who were on the stage with King Lear showed every inclination of taking an early curtain call. They moved close to the wings, where they could beat a hasty retreat if necessary. Lear still held his position in the centre of the stage.

> ' "I killed the slave that was a-hanging thee. Did I not, fellow?
> I have seen the day I would have made them skip—" '

'Let's see you skip then.' The cowboy who had drawn his gun, started to fire at the actor's feet. At the first sight of bullets hitting the makeshift stage the other two actors disappeared into the wings with alacrity. King Lear held his ground.

More than that he continued with his performance, missing out the section where the two
characters would have had speeches.

    ' "Why should a dog, a horse, a rat have life,
    And thou no breath at all?
    Thou'lt come no more,
    Never, never, never, never, never, never." '

The cowboy, visibly annoyed that he had failed
to drive the actor from the stage, said, 'You should
have gone when I told you. This time I'll singe
your whiskers.'

He fired a couple of shots which obviously went
dangerously close to the actor's head.

'Frank, for God's sake, let's get out of here,'
Cordelia whispered to King Lear.

Frank Lowry hesitated, he hated to be forced to
leave the stage by a drunken cowboy. The
audience was now restless. Some of them had
stood up. He obviously wasn't going to be given
the chance to finish the play. Another bullet
thudding into the canvas behind him made up his
mind. He was about to put Cordelia on her feet so
that they could leave the stage when the real
tragedy happened. A bullet hit her. Blood began
spreading over her white gown. Frank realized
with sickening horror that his Cordelia really was
dead.

* * *

The service was a simple one. The only ones attending were the theatrical troupe. There were eight of them in all. They were burying her in the town cemetery where a variety of crudely carved crosses testified to the high mortality rate among its few hundred inhabitants. They sang the hymn 'Nearer my God to Thee', before they laid her to rest. Ambrose, the odd-job man, had carved the details on the wooden cross. It read:

[Mary Lowry. 1866 – 1889. Actress.]

The cemetery was about half a mile away from the town. After Frank had laid his posy of flowers on the grave, the rest of the troupe walked in silence back to their two wagons, which were nearby. Frank stayed behind. The terrible anger which he had felt last night when his Mary had been killed by the drunken cowboy was gnawing at his innards. He knew it would not go away until he had avenged his wife's death. Not only her death, but their unborn child's as well, since she had been three months pregnant.

The cowboy's face was indelibly printed in his memory. It was a thin face with a weak jaw. The face was topped by bushy ginger hair and he was clean shaven. His name he had learned from Sam Steed, who had promoted the play, was Sol Wesley. He was the only son of Tasker Wesley who owned the Lone T, a big ranch to the west of the town. Tasker not only owned the farm, but he also owned the two saloons, the livery stable, and the Corn Store. 'In fact,' Sam, concluded, 'you could say he owns Langdon.'

He had asked about the law. This had brought a snort of laughter from Sam. 'Tasker is the law. There isn't any law around here. In fact I'm getting out of town now. My position isn't a very healthy one, since I'm a witness to a killing. There's no way that Tasker will have his son brought to justice. One way of making sure that that won't happen is to get rid of any witnesses pretty damned quick. Since you're another of the witnesses, I'd advise you to do the same.'

'What about the audience?' Frank had persisted. 'They were witnesses.'

'Most of them are tenant farmers. They rent their farms from Tasker. They do as they're told, or he will drive them from their farms.'

Frank finally returned to his wagon, which he shared with the other four men in the troupe. Clayton was already up on the driving-seat, with the reins in his hand, waiting to start.

'I'm not coming,' Frank announced.

'What?' Clayton looked down in massive disbelief.

Peter, who had heard the statement, appeared from inside the wagon. He was joined by the other two men. Finally the women joined in. The whole troupe tried to get him to change his mind. They argued and cajoled for half an hour, but he was adamant. They tried flattery: 'You are our best actor. What will we do without you?' It was to no avail.

Finally they gave in. They discussed the financial implications. 'We owe you a hundred dollars,' said Archie, the treasurer. 'That's your share and Mary's,' he concluded, with embarrassment.

'I'll take fifty. And one of the ponies.' He was referring to the two spare ponies which were tied to the back of the wagons. 'You can easily get another one when you hit the next town.'

'Why don't you buy one from the livery stable?' asked Clayton.

'I've got my reasons.'

It was young Alice who ventured the question which the others had been dying to ask. 'What are you going to do in Langdon?'

'I'm going to kill Sol Wesley,' he replied.

TWO

Frank's first visit was to the Lone T ranch. He hoped he would not come across Sol Wesley. If he did, he doubted whether he would be able to keep the hatred from his face.

He rode into the farm under the watchful eyes of two of Tasker Wesley's henchmen, Sy Drake and Hank Kimberly. Frank noticed that both men wore their gun-belts low – ready for an instant draw. He dismounted from his sorrel mare and tied her to the hitching rail.

'Howdee,' he said, amicably.

The two watchers had noted that he was not carrying a gun. 'What can we do for you, stranger?' asked Sy.

'I've come to see Mr Wesley.'

'Have you got a name?'

Frank had decided to conceal his name, since it had been displayed on billboards advertising the theatre's productions. 'Yeah. Al.'

Hank looked up from the stick he had been

whittling. 'Have you got another monniker?'

'Cornwall.'

'Al Cornwall.' Hank repeated slowly.

'What do you want to see Mr Wesley about?' demanded Sy.

'That's my business,' said Frank, giving them a friendly smile.

'Suppose we make it our business.' Hank had finished whittling. He looked along the length of stick as though he were sighting a gun.

Frank was determined not to show his irritation. The last thing he wanted was to fall at the first hurdle. It was imperative that he talked with Wesley. 'If you must know, I'm looking for a job.'

This brought a reaction from the two, and they studied him closely. 'You're not a cowhand,' said Sy, finally.

'Nope.'

'And you're not a gunman,' said Hank. The remark brought a smile to Sy's face. Hank glanced at Sy and smiled himself.

Frank noted with relief that the atmosphere seemed to have thawed. The initial suspicion had been replaced by a more relaxed atmosphere. Hank resumed his whittling.

'Can I see him?' asked Frank.

'Nope,' said Sy.

'Why not?'

'Because he's out on the range,' said Sy, with more than a hint of triumph in his voice.

14

Frank sighed. He realized now that they had been toying with him. The thing to do though was not to reveal any sign of irritation; join in the joke; share their smiles. 'So, when will he be back?' he asked casually, as though he had all the time in the world.

'Tomorrow,' Hank informed him.

As Frank rode away, he reflected that things hadn't got off to a very auspicious start. He had hoped to see Wesley, get a job, and then get some digs. Now he would have to change his plans and get the digs first.

Of course he could always stay at one of the two saloons, he reflected, as he rode back into Langdon. The trouble was he didn't like saloons – they generally attracted the wrong type of people. In spite of his reservations, he tied his horse to the hitching rail in front of the first saloon he came to and went inside and ordered a beer.

The barman who served him did not seem particularly interested in the newcomer, he was more interested in the game of poker which was going on at a nearby table.

'Will you have a drink yourself?' asked Frank, in an effort to grab his attention.

'Thanks, I'll have a whiskey.' The barman reluctantly turned his attention to Frank. 'Travelling through?'

'No, I'm thinking of staying. In fact I'm looking for digs. Is there anywhere you can recommend?'

The barman scratched his stubbled chin. 'I don't rightly know....'

One of the card-players who had dropped out of the hand they were playing, approached the bar. 'Feller here who's looking for digs,' the barman told the card-player. 'Anyone you can recommend, Saul?'

'Well, there's old Mrs Tiller. I hear she's looking for a lodger now that her son Matthew has left town. Her husband, Nathan, died a couple of months back,' the card-player informed Frank.

Frank received instructions how to reach the Tiller house. It was at the other end of town. He rode there and hitched his horse in front of a small neat house.

'Looking for digs?' the white-haired, middle-aged woman who had answered his knock examined him closely. He smiled encouragingly at her. He always got on well with elderly ladies. There was no answering smile from Mrs Tiller whose lined face was at the moment set in stern lines. 'You'd better come in.'

She led him into the front room. The furniture consisted of a sofa, an easy chair and a sideboard. On the sideboard were several glass cases of stuffed animals and birds. 'It was my late husband Nathan's hobby,' she announced, as she waved him to a seat.

He sat on the easy chair, which although old, was quite comfortable. 'Now, you say you are looking for lodgings, Mr—?'

'Cornwall. Al Cornwall.' He stood up to shake hands.

She studied him in silence for a few moments. 'It's a risky business – a widow taking a lodger, Mr Cornwall.'

He waited for her to conclude her inspection. 'I'm afraid I can't give you any references.'

'Oh, I don't believe in references. I believe in my own judgement. I will have to ask you some questions in order to satisfy myself, if that's all right with you?'

'Sure.'

'Are you married?'

'No,' he answered truthfully.

'Where do you come from?'

'Chicago.'

'What brings you so far West?'

'I don't know. The sense of freedom, I suppose.'

'Huh, some freedom here,' she retorted, scornfully. 'With Tasker Wesley controlling everything.'

'You don't like him …' Frank ventured.

'I hate him,' she said, venomously. Frank waited for an explanation. 'You'll learn why,' she continued more evenly. 'If you stay in the town any length of time.'

Oh. I aim to do just that, thought Frank, as they discussed the terms of payment for his lodgings.

THREE

The following day Frank again rode out to the Lone T ranch. This time he took more notice of the small farms that he passed. Most of the buildings were just shanties, with a garden in the front containing some vegetables, and by its side a single field in which wheat was growing. The wheat was ripening to a mellow golden colour and would obviously soon be ready for harvesting. In addition to their fields of corn, most of the small farmers had a few livestock – usually a couple of cows, a pig, and some chickens. Some of the farmers were working in their fields and gave him a friendly wave as he passed.

This time Tasker was in. Frank was shown into the study by Sy Drake. It was a fairly large room with an extensive collection of books bound mostly in red morocco. In the centre of the room was an impressive mahogany desk. Seated behind it was Tasker Wesley.

He was a handsome grey-haired man whom

Frank could imagine playing the role of one of the kings in Shakespeare's plays. He had a weather-beaten face, keen grey eyes and a firm jaw. Frank compared him with his son and he could find no similarity of feature.

'Sit down, Mr—?'

'Cornwall. Al Cornwall.' Frank sat down in a well-upholstered chair. He was aware of Tasker's keen gaze studying him.

'What can I do for you?'

Frank had prepared his speech. 'I'm travelling West, looking for somewhere to settle, and I thought I'd give Langdon a try. It seems to be the sort of growing town that I would like to settle in. It seems to have a future. I asked around for a job and was told that I should come to see you.'

'Whoever you asked gave you the right advice, young man. I am the person to see. I run the town. You might think that's a bit of an exaggeration, but I can assure you that it isn't. So you need a job?' Frank was once more aware of Tasker's gaze as he summed him up. 'What jobs can you do?'

'I'm not a cowhand—'

'I didn't think you were.' Tasker dismissed that suggestion with a wave of his hand.

'But I've been a teacher, served behind a bar, worked in a grocery store, worked in a livery stable—'

'All right. I get the picture.' Tasker stroked his chin thoughtfully. 'You say you've worked in a grocery store?'

'Yeah. My aunt keeps a grocery store in Chicago. I've helped out from time to time.'

'So you're good at figures?'

'I think so.'

Tasker nodded thoughtfully. 'Maybe I've got a job for you.' Frank waited for him to come to the point. 'It's a job for somebody I could trust. How do I know I can trust you?'

'You don't.'

'No, I don't, do I? Well, let me put it this way, if you let me down, or try to double-cross me, or cheat me, there'll be an unmarked grave in the cemetery. Do I make myself clear?'

The fact that Tasker issued the threat in such a matter-of-fact manner made it all the more chilling. 'Yes,' said Frank, aware that his mouth had suddenly become dry.

'Before we go into details, I'd better know if you're in trouble with the law. The last thing I want is some out-of-town lawman poking his nose around here.'

'I've never been in trouble with the law in my life,' Frank asserted.

Tasker was again studying him. 'All right,' he said finally. 'The job is working in the Corn Store. You saw it in town?' Frank nodded. 'The person in charge is Nat Hardy. He's getting a bit too old for the job. His eyesight isn't what it used to be. You'll be his assistant. You'll help in the store, but one of your main jobs will be to keep the accounts. Do you think you can do that?'

'I'm sure I can.'

'Keeping the accounts is very important.'

'You mean because most of the customers are given credit?'

'I mean because we don't use cash. We use tokens.' Tasker permitted himself a smile at Frank's surprise.

'You don't use cash at all?'

'Oh, some of the townfolk pay in cash, but most of the trading is done by my tenants. They pay in tokens. You'll soon get the hang of it.'

'So say someone comes in to buy a hundredweight of oats, then they'll give me tokens to the value of the goods.'

'That's right. Maybe you're wondering why we use tokens when it seems easier to use real money.'

'The thought had crossed my mind.'

Tasker allowed himself another thin smile. 'Basically it's to make sure that my tenants spend the money they earn in my stores, or in my saloons, or in my livery stable. It's to stop them riding into the next town and spending their money there.'

'What do these tokens look like?'

Tasker picked up a thin copper-coloured token which had been lying on his desk. He tossed it to Frank, who caught it. 'That's the dollar token.'

Frank examined it. It had the figure one stamped on it. 'You'll soon get used to them.'

Frank put it back on the desk. 'There's one thing I'd like to ask.'

'What's that?'

'Do I get paid in those or in real money?'

This time Tasker gave a wide smile. 'You'll get paid in real money, Cornwall. As long as I'm satisfied you're doing your job properly.'

FOUR

It was a thoughtful Frank who rode back into town. Tasker certainly seemed to have everything neatly sewn up. The reason for him staying in Langdon – to avenge the death of his lovely Mary – seemed more impossible in the cold light of today's meeting. Tasker obviously had several skilled gunmen at his beck and call, whereas he wasn't even carrying a gun. For a while as he rode along the dusty trail, he was tempted to forget the whole idea. If he hurried he could catch the actors' wagons before they left Wilton. His horse had slowed down as if in response to his indecision.

No. He'd stay. What had he got to lose? Nobody in the town knew him – that was a major factor on his side. He had been wearing thick white whiskers when he had been on stage, and since the actors hadn't mingled with the townsfolk, he was sure his identity was safe. He now had a job which, sometime in the future, would bring him into contact with Sol Wesley. As he often did,

Frank came up with an apt Shakespearean quotation. This was from one of his favourite characters, Othello, who, after having Cassio killed, says: 'Had all his hairs been lives, my great revenge had stomach for them all.'

His great revenge. He liked the sound of the phrase. He kicked his horse into a gallop.

Nat Hardy had a pleasant face with receding hair. He was wearing a dirty grey overall. He peered at Frank. 'You say you come from Tasker?'

'That's right. I've got a note here.' Frank produced it.

Nat took it. Studied it. Then handed it back to Frank. 'I can see it's in his handwriting. But I can't rightly read what's in it. The light isn't too good in here. Would you be so kind as to read it for me?'

Frank couldn't see anything wrong with the light. Still, he obliged. ' "The person carrying this note is Al Cornwall. You are to take him on as your helper. If he shapes up he'll become your regular helper." It's signed Tasker Wesley.'

Nat took the note and stuffed it in the pocket of his overalls. 'You worked in a corn store before?'

'No. But I've worked in a general store.'

'Where was that?'

'Chicago.'

Nat grunted. He studied Frank keenly. 'Some of these sacks are heavy. You don't look as though you've got much meat on you.'

26

'I can manage. I'm stronger than I look.' It was true. Much of the work off-stage involved carrying furniture from one of their wagons to the stage-door and setting it up. Even on stage he had to hold Cordelia in his arms for a lengthy spell while he delivered his speeches.

Nat grunted again. 'We'll see. When do you aim to start?'

'Now.'

Nat grinned showing broken teeth. 'You're keen, ain't you?'

'I need the money.'

'In that case, welcome.' He extended a gnarled hand which Frank shook.

Nat took him on an inspection of the shop. 'I suppose you know the difference between corn, oats and barley?'

'Yeah.'

'Right. That's most of the stuff we sell. We also sell seeds, some newfangled stuff called fertilizer – as if dung isn't good enough, bales of hay….' Nat took him into the back of the store where a lot of the produce was stored. It had the distinctive sweet dry smell of stores that carried a lot of seed. Nat stopped by a bag of corn. He picked out one of the grains. 'See that?' He held the ripe grain in his hand. 'We only stock the best. Tasker sees to that. If any of the farmers try to pass off any poor stuff, he soon gets rid of them.' He put the grain in his mouth and began to chew it.

'How many tenant farmers are there?'

'Seventeen. I'll give you the list. They always pay in tokens.'

'I know.'

A woman's voice shouted from inside the shop. 'Nat, where the hell are you?'

They went out. Standing there was an attractive young woman. She was a redhead with the perfect complexion some redheads have. She was wearing an expensive frock which Frank would have expected to see in Boston rather than in Langdon. To an actor and stage manager who was used to summing up pretty faces, Frank decided that hers was quite pretty, but rather spoiled by weak, pouty lips.

'Where the hell have you been? You're supposed to be serving customers, not skulking in the back.'

'I'm sorry, Miss Laurie. What can I get you?'

Frank was surprised at the servile way in which Nat spoke to her.

'I want some seed for my birds.'

Nat went over to an open sack and began to scoop some into a bag. The young lady studied Frank coolly, leaning insolently on her parasol. Frank held her stare. Nat returned with the seed, breaking the tension. 'Will that be all, Miss Laurie?'

'For now.' She flashed a final insolent glance at Frank before turning on her heel.

Nat sighed with relief as she left the store.

'A special customer?' guessed Frank.

'The less I see of her the better.'

'What's her name?'

'Laurie Wesley. She's Tasker Wesley's daughter.'

FIVE

Despite Frank's protestations that the hard work of lifting the sacks of grain wouldn't bother him, he soon found that he had exaggerated his own fitness. Every day he had to carry several of the hundredweight sacks from the back of the store, out through the side door. He then had to lift them up on to the waiting wagons.

In the beginning Nat would watch him with a knowing grin. Frank usually managed it without spilling too much grain. He also managed to hide the fact that his muscles were screaming in protest at the exertion.

In the evening, he would return to Mrs Tiller's neat house. There, a dinner, usually stew with plenty of dumplings in it, would be waiting for him. Although the meal was excellent, the thing he enjoyed most came after Mrs Tiller had gone to bed. She always went to bed early, leaving him alone in the kitchen. He would have already filled the big copper kettle on the fire, then, when she had gone to bed, he would get the tin bath down from its hook on the wall. He would fill it with the steaming water and luxuriously soak his aches and pains away.

'I've never known anyone take so many baths, Mr Cornwall,' Mrs Tiller observed one morning, at breakfast.

'Cleanliness is next to godliness,' said Frank, with a serious face.

She glanced at him suspiciously, as though trying to decide whether he was teasing her.

One evening, after dinner, he broached the subject of Tasker Wesley. 'There are a lot of people in town who don't like him ...' he ventured.

She was poking the fire. At the mention of Tasker's name she gave the fire a vicious poke, spraying a shower of sparks over the grate. 'I'd better not say too much against him, since you're working for him,' she said, finally.

'As far as I'm concerned, it's just a job. I don't owe him any loyalty.'

She nodded. 'Well, that's as maybe. Anyhow, you're bound to find out, sooner or later.'

'Find out what?'

She turned her attention away from the grate to face him. 'We were tenant farmers of Tasker. We had the usual smalholding. Nathan worked hard keeping it up to scratch. We had been there two years when Nathan and some of the farmers got together. They decided they had had enough of being paid in tokens and wanted to be paid in real money so that they could go to Wilton or even Drakesville and buy their own grain at fair prices, instead of being forced to buy it at Tasker's store, at the price he set.'

She turned her attention to poking the fire. Frank wisely kept his silence. He knew there was more to come.

'They elected Nathan to be their spokesman. Although most of the time he was a quiet man, he could be quite....' She searched for the word.

'Eloquent,' suggested Frank.

'Yes, eloquent. He was a good speaker. So they picked him to go to Tasker and explain that they wanted to be paid in cash.'

'What happened?'

'I'll tell you what happened.' Her voice rose. 'Tasker laughed in his face.'

'So he didn't succeed?'

'Oh, Nathan succeeded all right. He succeeded in getting himself killed.'

'What happened?'

'You ask too many questions,' she snapped. She stood up. Her attitude indicated that Frank was not going to get the answer to his question tonight. She busied herself with the usual tasks of bolting the doors and winding the clock. She didn't even say goodnight to him as she climbed the narrow stairs.

At work the following day Frank tried to find

out what happened from Nat. He wasn't very forthcoming either.

'Better to let sleeping dogs lie,' was his advice.

Gradually Frank's muscles were getting used to the new demands put on them in hoisting and carrying the heavy sacks. He had also adjusted to the enquiring stares he received from the tenant farmers until Nat introduced him. Most of the farmers shook hands with him and their greeting on the surface seemed pleasant enough, but Frank thought he detected an undercurrent of hostility. Finally he broached the subject with Nat.

'Stands to reason they're not keen on you,' Nat informed him. 'They see you as one of Tasker's men.'

The irony of the situation was not lost on Frank. That night as he soaked in his bath he reflected that it would have been a good theme for a dramatist. Here he was, with his avowed aim of killing Sol Wesley, and yet the tenant farmers regarded him as their enemy – one of Tasker's men, in fact.

At the end of the first fortnight Tasker came into the store once. He nodded briefly to Frank then went into the back room with Nat. Frank guessed that he might be their subject of conversation.

This was confirmed when Tasker came out ten minutes later. This time there was a smile on his face. 'Nat tells me you're shaping up well,' he announced.

'I hope so.'

'In the circumstances I think we can say that you are now a regular member of my staff.'

'Thanks.'

'I want you to take the wagon to Wilton tomorrow to pick up some supplies.'

'Certainly.'

Tasker gave him a thoughtful stare before turning on his heel. Frank was breathing a sigh of relief that the interview seemed to have gone well, when Tasker turned at the door. 'There's one other thing: my daughter, Laurie, will be coming with you. She wants to do some shopping in Wilton.'

Frank received the information with outward calm. 'I'll be pleased to accompany her,' he said. But Tasker was already going out through the door.

Nat had heard the exchange. 'You want to watch her,' he said, having made sure that Tasker was indeed out of earshot.

'Why do you say that?'

'She's poison,' said Nat, emphatically.

SIX

The following morning Frank rode out to the ranch. It was a fine morning and a song-bird was singing melodically from the top of a gorse bush as he passed. He reflected that it would be a perfect day, except for one thing: Miss Laurie would be accompanying him.

He had asked Nat what he had meant about her being poison. At first Nat was not very forth-coming. Finally, when they were having their midday snack, he opened out.

'She's been spoiled rotten by her father. Her mother died when she was born, so she's had no mother to keep her in control. Just a lot of nannies. They've come and gone on the ranch like summer birds. Some of them only stayed a day.' Nat spat at an iron weight, hitting it unerringly.

'How old is she?'

'Oh, I dunno. About twenty-three, twenty-four.'

'It's a wonder she isn't married.'

'Oh, she was. To a feller named Grainger. I can't

rightly recollect his first name.' He scratched his stubbled chin.

'What happened to him?'

'He was found hanging from a beam in one of their barns.'

'Somebody killed him?'

'They all said he'd hanged himself. They stuck to their story. There's no sheriff here. And the nearest marshal is thirty miles away, in Drakesville.'

'What did the doctor say who examined him?'

'Old Doctor Rawlings? He's a big friend of the family. He said there were rope burns on the man's hands.'

'Which suggests that he had changed his mind and tried to untie the knot. But it was too late.'

'That's what Doctor Rawlings said.' Nat spat again. This time hitting one of the smaller weights.

'But if it wasn't suicide, and it was murder, why should she want him killed?'

Nat glanced around fearfully at the mention of the word murder, even though the shop was closed. 'The talk was that she was playing around.'

'She had another boy-friend?'

'Several. So they say.'

'But why have her husband killed?'

'He used to beat her.'

'Ah!' It was an expressive 'Ah!' the sort of 'Ah!'

that signified that the recipient had guessed the whole story.

It still seemed a bit drastic though, Frank reflected, as he drew up outside the ranch. Laurie's white mare was saddled up and she was standing by it, impatiently tapping her crop against her thigh. 'Where the hell have you been?' she snapped. 'I've been waiting for half an hour.'

'I didn't know what time we were starting,' Frank pointed out.

'Well next time, make sure you get here early.'

'Yes, ma'am.'

She was wearing a red shirt and jodpurs. She had a green scarf tied round her neck and her red hair was pinned back in a bun. Frank had to admit that she looked very attractive, even though she was pouting with annoyance. But she was definitely a young lady not to get mixed up with.

He was glad to see that she was riding a horse. If she had been accompanying him on the wagon, he would have been forced to make conversation. As it was she rode a few yards ahead, leaving him to indulge in his own thoughts.

He hoped that he would be able to turn the journey to Wilton to his own favour. There was something he was keen on purchasing. There was no problem in purchasing it in Langdon except that it would soon become common knowledge, since the hardware store he would be buying it from was owned by Tasker. And word would inevitably get back to him. Tasker might start wondering why an apparently inoffensive, peaceful person like Al Cornwall would suddenly want a gun.

After a while, Laurie dropped back so that she was now riding alongside the wagon. From time to time she glanced across at him. He felt that he had to be polite and start a conversation.

'Are you planning to do much shopping in Wilton?'

'Not much.'

'I've got to call in the store. Maybe we can arrange to meet somewhere after?'

'Maybe.'

He wanted at least an hour to himself. That would give him time to pick up the provisions. And then go to the hardware store to select a pistol. He tried to start the conversation again. 'I've never been to Wilton.'

'It's bigger than Langdon.'

End of conversation, he thought. However she followed it up with a useful piece of information. 'There's a hotel. It's named the Grand. After I've finished shopping I'll be there in the lounge. Have you got that?'

'Yes, ma'am.'

'And don't keep me waiting.'

She took up her position a few yards in front of the wagon. It reminded him of something he had read about the Royal Family in London. In the magazine it had stated that when Queen Victoria went out with her husband, he was always a few paces behind her – since she was the queen and he was only a prince. This was just the same, he thought, wryly. The queen was riding in front.

They reached Wilton without mishap, and without indulging in any further conversation. They were riding down the main street, with Laurie still leading, when a woman's voice called out from the sidewalk. At first Frank didn't realize that the person was calling out to him. Then, when he heard his name being called, his heart sank.

'Frank. Frank Lowry.'

It was young Alice. She was skipping along the sidewalk trying to keep up with the wagon.

He ignored her. He tried to get the horse pulling the wagon to go faster. But it was very much a one-speed horse, and it ignored his jerking on the rein.

'Frank. It's me. Alice.'

He was aware that he was the object of attention of two women. Not only was Alice waving frantically at him but Laurie had turned in her saddle and was regarding him quizzically.

SEVEN

As he stopped outside the store Frank mentally cursed the bad luck which had brought him to the same place at the same time as Alice. Laurie was tying her horse to the rail. Alice had dropped back on the sidewalk after apparently failing to attract his attention. He did not know whether she was planning another assault on his memory, or whether she had given up in disgust since he had pointedly ignored her.

Laurie approached him. Frank groaned inwardly. Here it was. All his plans were about to be shattered.

'That young lady seemed to know you.'

There was only one thing to do. Try to bluff it out. 'What young lady?'

'The one who was running alongside the wagon. You couldn't have missed her. She kept waving to you.'

'She was calling somebody else's name. I didn't take any notice of her.' His throat had gone dry.

43

'She seemed positive that she knew you.'

'She must have been mistaken. I've got an ordinary face. I've been mistaken for somebody else before now.'

'What did she keep calling you? Frank. Frank Lowry.'

'That shows she must have been mistaken.' Their eyes locked. He knew that she was trying to discover the slightest sign that he was lying. His years on the stage stood him in good stead. He was used to putting on a mask in front of an audience in order to convince them that the author's words were real. Now it was imperative that he convince Laurie that he was telling the truth.

He thought he detected a flicker of indecision in her gaze. 'So you've no idea who this Frank Lowry is?' she demanded, finally.

'No. None.'

He breathed a huge sigh of relief as she finally turned on her heel and headed towards one of the ladies' outfitters.

He went into the store and placed his order. 'Can you put them on the wagon for me? I've got another call to make.'

'They're for Tasker Wesley?'

'That's right.' If Frank was surprised that the young man behind the counter should know about Tasker in this town he hid his surprise.

'I recognized Miss Laurie,' the assistant confided.

So that was it. It was Miss Laurie who was known in the store. After all, why shouldn't she be? She probably came in to Wilton regularly. Especially since there was obviously very little in the form of amusement or recreation for a young lady in Langdon.

Frank's next call was at the hardware store. A middle-aged man with a thin, watchful face stood behind the counter. 'How can I help you?'

'I want a pistol. A Colt.'

He turned and went to a rack behind the counter on which Frank could see a number of guns. 'How about this?'

It was a beautiful gun, black with ivory inset plates. The store-keeper had noticed Frank's eyes light up when he had taken it from the rack. 'Try it.'

Frank held it in his hand. It was perfectly balanced. His finger curved over the trigger as though it had been tailored for him.

'How much?'

'You want the belt and holster?'

'Yeah.'

'Twenty dollars. Bullets extra.'

'I'll take it.' Frank also bought a couple of boxes of bullets.

'Aiming to do some shooting?' asked the store-keeper, with a friendly smile, as he laid the purchases in front of Frank.

'Thinking about it. Could you do me a favour?'

'What is it?'

'Could you wrap them all up in a parcel for me?' The last thing he wanted was for Laurie to see the pistol. She was probably already wondering whether Al Cornwall was who he said he was. But she would conclude that at least he appeared to be a peaceful person. Not the sort who you would expect any trouble from. If she saw his purchases it would really set her thinking. And the next step would probably be to report to her father that the person working in his corn store was really a wolf in sheep's clothing.

While the store-keeper was parcelling up his purchases, Frank put an apparently innocent question to him. 'I understand there's an acting company in town.'

'Yeah. They've been putting on some plays in the Lyceum. Don't bother much with plays myself.'

'You don't know when they're leaving?'

'Sure. Today. I've got a billboard in the front window. If you want to catch their play, then you're unlucky.'

Frank thanked him absentmindedly. It was a stroke of bad luck, Alice seeing him earlier. She had probably been on her way to their wagons – just picking up a few purchases before they pulled out. If he and Laurie had come in tomorrow, then their meeting wouldn't have taken place. And the seeds of doubt wouldn't have been sown in Laurie's mind.

Frank collected his other purchases from the general store and carefully hid his own parcel underneath the sacks. The visits to the two stores had taken longer than he would have wished. Still there was nothing for it, but to go to the hotel and to face Laurie's wrath once again.

He found her in the foyer. She was sitting alone with a glass of lemonade in front of her. She glanced up as he entered.

'Is everything all right?' To his surprise she gave him a welcoming smile. It confirmed his first impression of her, that she could be a very attractive young woman.

'Yeah.'

'Have you had anything to drink?'

'No.'

She beckoned to a passing waiter. 'Bring me another glass,' she commanded peremptorily.

When the glass was brought she poured a glass of lemonade from the jug on the table. She handed it to Frank.

'Thanks,' he said. He wondered why she had suddenly changed in her attitude towards him. On the way into town her demeanour had either been one of hostility, or she had ignored him completely. She had changed drastically. She gave him a friendly smile as he drank his lemonade. He couldn't help but remember Nat's advice: 'She's poison'. As she glanced casually around at the others seated at the tables, Frank

47

studied her. She was completely relaxed with none of the tension of someone with fluctuating moods which he had observed before. In fact she looked pleased with herself – like the cat who had got the cream. Her very casualness made Frank uneasy. I may be wrong, he thought, but I think it bodes trouble.

They set off on their return journey. To Frank's relief, Laurie still rode ahead of him and he studied her back as she sat straight in the saddle. She was a natural horsewoman, who had been brought up among horses, and had the lithe movements of a cowhand. He knew she could outride him, if it ever came that they were matched against each other. Some of her red hair had escaped from the bun and had strayed down her neck. He noted that it was a shapely neck. He switched his attention away from her and flicked the reins to make his horse keep up with her. The last thing he wanted was to be the object of one of her flashes of annoyance.

They were about a mile away from the ranch when Laurie called a halt. A puzzled Frank pulled up alongside. 'Is everything all right,' he demanded.

'I'm just going to give my horse some water.' They had stopped by a stream.

Since they had only a mile to go, Frank wondered about her decision to stop. However, he said nothing, and watched while she dismounted.

48

While the horse was drinking she came alongside the wagon. It was obvious to Frank that she was going to engage him in conversation. He prayed silently that it wasn't going to be about young Alice calling him Frank Lowry.

To his relief she started talking about Langdon. How it was a one-horse town with nothing to do there. 'Not unless you go to the saloon. Do you go to the saloon, Al?'

'No, I'm not much of a drinking man.'

She studied him. 'No, I didn't think you were. So what do you do in the evenings?'

'I read,' said Frank, truthfully.

'We've got a lot of books in the house.'

'I know. I've seen them.'

'Who's your favourite author?'

'I like Charles Dickens. The English writer.'

'We've got a complete set of his books. Why don't you call sometime. You can borrow which ones you like.'

'Thanks. I will.'

She returned to her horse which had drunk its fill. She climbed up into the saddle and they set off as before. Frank congratulated himself on having come unscathed from the conversational exchange with her. She had obviously accepted his explanation that young Alice had been mistaken about his identity. He let his mind wander to the collection of books he had seen in her house. The quick glance that he had been able to bestow on it

49

had shown him that it was an excellent collection. Maybe he would take her up on her suggestion that he could borrow some of the books.

She drew up in front of the ranch. Frank turned round the back and pulled up outside the barn where he started to unload the wagon. There was nobody else in sight. He guessed that the farmhands were in the kitchen having their chow. The thought of food made him realize that he was hungry, too. Never mind, he would soon be having a good, hot meal cooked by his landlady.

He stabled the horse. He had transferred the parcel containing the pistol to his own saddle-bag and was leading it out of the stables when Laurie appeared round the corner. He had assumed that she had gone into the house.

To his surprise she stood in front of him, blocking his way. Short of leading the horse round her there was nothing he could do but stop. She held something in her hand. It was a sheet of paper. Frank's heart sank as he recognized it as one of the dozens of billboards posted round Langdon.

'I think you owe me an explanation, Frank Lowry,' she said, coldly.

EIGHT

During the next few days Frank went over and over Laurie's confrontation. When she had presented him with the handbill he had realized immediately there was no point in trying to keep up the pretence that he was not Frank Lowry. He put a brave face on it and admitted that he was the actor.

Her next question was why was he pretending to be Al Cornwall? He had to think quickly. He came up with the only answer he could think of on the spur of the moment, namely that he was Al Cornwall.

This took her aback. She subjected him to one of her long stares. Finally she had enquired, in that case why should he want to change his name?

He explained that actors frequently changed their names. If they were born with an ordinary name, and felt that a better sounding name would help them in promoting themselves, then they just changed their names.

This was something new to her. He wasn't sure whether he had convinced her or not. She chewed on her lower lip while she absorbed the information. Finally she asked him to name an actor who had changed his name.

He named the only actor who came to mind – Henry Irving. She told him that she had never heard of him. He explained that he was a famous actor from England who had recently toured the United States. He added that his name was really John Brodribb.

At this stage he could see that she was half-convinced by his explanation. He was congratulating himself on getting neatly out of a tricky situation when she sprang her next question: why did he ignore the young lady who was shouting at him in Wilton?

Again he had to think quickly. He advanced the only answer he could think of, that he had quarrelled with the company. In fact, he added, that was why he had stayed in Langdon.

What had they quarrelled about?

Oh, one of the things that actors quarrel about from time to time – where they were going to put on their next shows. He had wanted them to turn round and head back East while the rest of the company wanted to go West – on towards San Francisco.

What about the actress Sol killed? she had asked, casually.

It took massive will-power for him not to show any emotion. From her tone she might have been discussing her brother having killed a rabbit. He swore to himself that he would get even with the Wesley family – not only with his wife's murderer, but also with Laurie for the casual way she had referred to it.

She let him go shortly afterwards. He knew she would go over his answers to her questions when she was alone. All he had done was to buy time. He had allayed her suspicions for a short while but in the longer term he was realist enough to know that his deception could not be maintained. Sooner or later Laurie would find out that the woman who had been buried in the cemetery was his wife, Mary. Then it would simply be a matter of putting two and two together. And coming up with the answer that he had stayed in Langdon to avenge his wife's killing.

Nat noticed a change in his demeanour in the following days, so much so that he broached the subject. 'You've been mighty quiet since you returned from Wilton with Miss Laurie.'

'It's nothing to do with her,' he replied, quickly. 'I've been having trouble with a tooth.'

'There's nothing worse than toothache,' Nat agreed, sympathetically. 'If you want to have it out, there's a dentist in Wilton.'

'I'll have to wait 'til I go there next time.'

'Perhaps Miss Laurie will want you to go with

her again soon.'

If Nat thought that there was anything between him and Laurie, he couldn't be further from the truth, Frank thought, as he went to serve a customer.

Nat returned to the subject of Frank's tooth later. 'Of course, I could pull it out for you.'

Frank, who had no intention of having a perfectly good tooth pulled out, hastily declined the offer.

'Pity,' said Nat, regretfully. 'I've pulled out teeth before. I tie some thread round the tooth, then I tie it to the hoist. Then I let the hoist go. And the tooth comes out with it.'

'And it pulls your jaw out as well, I suppose,' said Frank, with a smile.

'I don't know about that. But at least it's cheered you up. That's the first time I've seen you smile for days.'

Frank confessed to himself that he didn't have much to smile about. He was planning to kill a man. It didn't exactly make him feel happy. The fact that Sol deserved to die did not make it any easier.

Every evening after dinner he would ride out to a deserted spot which he had found. He would don the holster and pistol and put up some empty tins on the old wall. They were about twenty paces away and at about the height of Sol's heart. Then he would draw the pistol, slipping the hammer, aiming and firing all in one movement.

The first few days he found that he only hit one or at the most, two of the tins. As far as speed of draw was concerned, he was quite happy with it. He had been in a stage play called 'Guns of the Wild West' where he had played the part of a sheriff who was supposed to clean up a town, killing all the bad guys. On the stage he had to draw his gun and shoot down two villians. At the end of the play's run of eight weeks, he had become an expert at drawing the gun quickly. The bullets he had fired on the stage had been blanks, but the gun had been the same Colt he was now using so it had a very familiar feel to it.

The stage show had been very popular back East. However, when they started moving West, they had found that the thin storyline and the unconvincing characters had not been too well received by the people in the townships. So they had decided to try a few of Shakespeare's plays. The result was a personal tragedy.

He had made a few trips to the cemetery. Each time he put a posy of flowers on Mary's grave. Each time it reinforced his resolve to avenge her death. It gave him the determination to carry on practising his shooting and his marksmanship gradually improved. As an actor he knew that practice was the key to any successful endeavour. He could now almost guarantee to hit three of the tins with the six bullets. On some occasions he had hit four. And once he had hit five.

His absence every evening finally caused a comment from Mrs Tiller. 'I see you've found somewhere to go in the evenings.'

He knew he couldn't tell her that he was practising shooting out on the range. There was only one other place he could think of where he could be spending his time. 'I go to the saloon. To play cards.'

'The Devil's cards,' she said, with a sniff. 'As long as you don't come in here with too much liquor inside you, it's up to you what you do with your money.'

He realized, rather sadly, that he had gone down in her estimation.

NINE

The day dawned when, inevitably, he came face to face with Sol Wesley. His first glimpse of him was when he saw Sol swagger through the door. Frank knew that if he had had his pistol in his belt he would have drawn it and to hell with the consequences, such was the hatred that surged up inside him.

Maybe he was lucky that Sol ignored him and went straight up to Nat, since Frank doubted whether he would have been able to keep the hatred from his face. Sol slapped down an order on the counter. 'Get this lot put up. Make sure they're ready by the time I come back or you'll be in trouble.' With that he turned on his heel and left.

'Nice manners the Tasker family have,' observed Nat, when Sol was out of earshot. To his surprise it did not bring a riposte from Frank. Nat turned to him and saw that he was staring at the door through which Sol had gone with an expression that Nat had never seen on his face before. It was an expression of such undiluted hatred that it made Nat shiver involuntarily.

They busied themselves making up the order. For the next few minutes they were too occupied for further conversation. The order completed, Nat leaned against the counter. He took out a tin of tobacco and some cigarette papers and rolled a cigarette, leaving the edge of the paper ready to be dampened down and rolled over to complete it. Instead of licking it himself, he offered it to Frank. This was the first occasion during the time Frank had been working in the store that Nat had offered him a smoke. Frank was about to refuse when he suddenly changed his mind. He took the cigarette, licked the edge of the paper, and finished rolling it. 'Thanks,' he said.

'It's none of my business,' said Nat, as he rolled another cigarette for himself, 'except that I don't like to see a nice boy like you get into trouble. Especially because of that no-good family, the Taskers.'

'I don't know what you're talking about,' said Frank, taking a pull on his cigarette.

'You went off with that she-devil of a daughter the other week. Since you've been back, you've gone so quiet I could get more talk out of a dead parrot. Then that skunk of a brother came in a few minutes ago. You should have seen your face when he left. If looks could kill he'd be on his way to the undertaker now. I don't know what's between you and the Tasker family – that's your own business – but whatever it is, I can tell you they're not worth it. Take the advice of an old man and keep away from them.'

'You've got it wrong,' said Frank, lamely.

'Have I?' Nat stared at him keenly.

Frank was saved from further discussion about the Tasker family by the arrival of a customer. Nat then gave Frank the task of sorting out some of the sacks. This kept him in the back room for some time. When he returned to the counter, he observed that Sol's order had vanished.

'He's been back then?' queried Frank.

'Yip,' said Nat, non-committally.

Frank guessed that Nat had sent him into the back room to avoid further confrontation. He didn't like deceiving the old man about his relationship with the younger Taskers, but there was nothing he could do about it at the moment. He resolved that as soon as he could he would put the record straight about his intentions towards Sol. But that wouldn't be in the foreseeable future.

It was several days later when he was confronted by Laurie. He was busy adding up some accounts when he was aware that someone had come into the shop. Nat was loading a wagon outside and there was no one else in the shop at the time. He was aware of her presence before she spoke. Maybe it was her perfume. Or perhaps it was just that he had been expecting her to come in.

'Hullo Frank. Or shall I call you Al?'

He looked up. She looked a picture in a wide-brimmed hat, a tight-fitting white dress and shoes that had somehow managed to escape the dust outside. She caught his appreciative glance and smiled knowingly. She moved up to the counter until they were within a few inches of each other.

He swallowed nervously. 'Al will do. Can I get you anything?'

'Oh, I don't want anything from the store.' She licked her lips provocatively.

'Oh? How can I help you, Miss Laurie?'

'Please call me Laurie.'

'Is there anything I can get you?' He tried to keep his tone neutral. He realized he wasn't too successful. Having such an attractive woman standing close to him was not conducive to casual conversation, particularly one who held all the cards.

She was enjoying his discomfort. 'I'll have a glass of water. It's hot travelling in the buckboard.'

So that was how she managed to look so immaculate, he realized, as he went into the back room to get some water. Nat was still outside, so there was no way he could appeal to him for help in dealing with the deadly member of the female species who was in the shop.

'Thanks.' For a few moments her hand covered his as he held out the glass. They stood like statues as she stared at him. 'I think we understand each other,' she said, as she finally accepted the glass.

Had she just come into the shop to toy with him, he wondered, as she sipped the water. To tell him, not in so many words, but nevertheless in an unmistakable manner that he was in her power? Had she visited the cemetery and seen the stark evidence of the wooden cross over the grave? He had been tempted to take it down on his last visit, in order to help conceal his identity. Then he had realized that it would be like desecrating the grave. No, the cross would stay there forever. No matter what happened to him.

'You said you liked reading.'

'Wh-at?' The sudden change of subject took him completely by surprise.

'You can borrow some books from our collection.'

'Th-anks,' he stammered out.

She smiled her secret smile. 'You'll come out this afternoon.'

'But I'll be working here.'

'I'll tell Nat to let you go.'

There was no way he could get out of it. The spider had the fly completely in its power. Her parting words dispelled any thoughts that it could be just a social visit. 'Daddy is away in Drakesville. He won't be back until tomorrow.'

TEN

Tasker Wesley was in fact visiting the county marshal. He had been summoned to see him by a letter which had arrived by stage. The letter had stated that the government was concerned about the lawlessness which was rife in the western states of the country. It added that they were determined to stamp it out. To that end it was incumbent on each township to appoint a sheriff and Tasker had been summoned to discuss the matter.

Marshal Smythe had been a major in the army before retiring to take up his present position. He still had the bushy moustache and side-whiskers which were favoured by many of the officers. However, since leaving the army, as the years had passed, so had his girth around the middle increased. He had some tales to tell of the Indian Wars in which he had fought. His florid complexion also told of his partiality to whiskey. He now offered Tasker a glass, which his visitor accepted.

'To the president.' The marshal raised his glass in a toast. Tasker did likewise.

'I haven't been to Langdon for a couple of years,' said the marshal, wiping his whiskers with the back of his hand. 'But I hear it's expanding.'

'Yes, it's growing,' Tasker agreed cautiously.

'It must be the women's fault. For having all those babies,' chortled the marshal. Tasker gave a false smile pretending appreciation of the joke.

'Well, now to business. I've got here a letter from the government in Washington.' The marshal tapped a letter importantly with his forefinger. 'It wants action. We must try to stamp out the lawlesness which is spreading West.'

He waited for a comment from Tasker. 'Yes, I agree,' the latter replied positively.

'Good. As the most influential citizen in Langdon I hope you will play your part.' He offered Tasker another drink, which he accepted.

'Anything that's in my power to keep law and order, you can depend on my help.'

'Excellent. Since we see eye to eye on the matter, we can discuss details. The first thing we need to do is to appoint a sheriff. Then afterwards we will need a town gaol.'

'A sheriff.' Tasker gave the impression that consideration of the matter had taken him by surprise, although he had half-guessed that it was the purpose of his summons to the marshal's office.

'The person appointed will be funded half by the county, and the other half must be found by the townsfolk.'

'I see.' Tasker scratched his chin reflectively.

'I know I've sprung this on you. I don't expect you to come up with a name straightaway.'

'Can this sheriff be anyone who's living in the town?'

'Yes. He doesn't have to have any previous experience. I think that would be asking too much.'

Tasker was still deep in thought. 'He would have to be a fairly young man?' he asked finally.

'I think that's definitely a necessity. He must be someone the townsfolk will respect. He shouldn't be a drunkard. Or have any criminal record.'

'There are three or four people who might fit the bill, but obviously I'll have to consult them first.'

'He must be a Christian – that goes without saying.'

'How much will he be paid?'

'A hundred dollars a month.'

'Does he have to be able to use a gun?'

'Yes. It's in the letter.' The marshal tapped the letter again. 'The sheriff is expected to wear a gun and to be able to use it in an emergency.'

Later, when he left the marshal's office, and he was having dinner in his hotel, Tasker went over the names of the three candidates he could put forward as future sheriff. All of them were controlled by him, but for one reason or another, none of them was exactly suitable. Of course, the other person who would be the ideal candidate would be Al Cornwall. He was one of his men. He had proved to be a very competent worker. Not only that but he had the indefinable quality of leadership and was quite young – probably still in his late twenties. It was a pity he couldn't use a gun; if he could, he would be the ideal candidate.

ELEVEN

Frank was in fact carrying a gun but he hadn't intended putting it on. He had returned to his lodgings to change out of his working clothes, and put on a suit, when the idea had suddenly struck him. Here he was going out to the Wesley farm. He knew that Tasker was away so presumably only Laurie and Sol were in residence. Perhaps this was his chance to avenge his wife's death. Perhaps today would be his chance to gun down Sol – just as he had gunned down his beloved Mary.

When he went downstairs, Mrs Tiller was busy in the kitchen. Her gaze took in the gun-belt and the pistol. 'I see you're going shooting,' she stated.

'Maybe.'

'There are a lot of vermin around.'

'So they say.'

'Nathan would never carry a gun.'

'Well, I don't usually carry one....'

'He should have carried one,' she said,

venomously. 'If he had, he might be alive today.'

There was no doubt that there was a connection between Nathan's death and the Wesleys Frank ruminated, as he rode towards the farm. Mrs Tiller had hinted at it on more than one occasion. She had stated that it was because Nathan had stood up to the Wesleys that he had met his demise. As he passed some of the tenant farmers working in their fields he wondered whether the Wesleys had Nathan killed because he had helped to unite the farmers in a single purpose – to get rid of the shackles imposed by Tasker.

He remembered reading in his history books about a group of farmers in England who had banded together to try to get better conditions from their landlord. He remembered their names: the Tolpuddle Martyrs. The trouble was he couldn't remember exactly what happened to them. The only thing he could assume was, since they were martyrs, they had met a violent death – probably by hanging.

He was so absorbed in his thoughts that he didn't notice the two riders until they had almost come alongside him. When he glanced up he saw that the riders were Sy and Hank and they kept pace with him as he rode along. They were the last pair he would have chosen as travelling companions.

Sy's first remark told him that they were going to carry on with the ribbing they had subjected him to the first time they had met. 'I wonder where the dude is going to, all dressed up?'

'And carrying a gun, too,' said Hank.

'Are you sure you know how to use that gun?' demanded Sy. 'Do you know which end is which?'

This brought a guffaw from Hank. Frank decided that his best policy was to keep silent. The farm was in sight and he had only about a quarter of a mile to go.

'He's not talking to us,' said Hank.

'That's not very sociable is it?' demanded Sy.

'What's the matter? Cat got your tongue?'

'I don't like people who won't even pass the time of day with us.'

'The dude thinks we're not good enough for him, that's what it is.'

'You reckon?' demanded Sy.

The farm was now only a couple of hundred yards away. Only another few minutes and he would be able to get rid of them. Hank had untied his lariat and was swinging it nonchalantly. 'We don't like anyone who ignores us.'

'Especially those who look down their noses at us,' supplied Sy.

'Especially those who look down their noses at us,' repeated Hank.

Frank was busy concentrating on closing the gap between himself and the farm which was now barely a hundred yards away, and so he didn't see it coming. One moment he was riding along comfortably, the next his arms were pinned to his side as the lariat snaked through the air. He had a split second to roll with the fall as he was jerked savagely from his horse.

'Well what do you know?' said Sy. 'He's fallen from his horse.'

Hank guffawed.

Frank regained his feet. Before he could try to loosen the rope around his arms, he was pulled forward. He stumbled and almost lost his footing. Because Hank kept his horse trotting forward, Frank was forced to run after them. Hank kept a tight hold on the lariat, forcing Frank to keep up with them until they reached the farm. Hank stopped his horse. After a brief struggle Frank managed to release himself.

'Perhaps that'll teach you to talk to us next time.'

'You've got guns,' said Frank.

There was a huge silence. Finally Hank said, 'He wants to play some more.'

They had dismounted and now moved slightly so that they were no longer side by side, but a few feet apart. Their hands were hanging down by their thighs.

Frank guessed that they were both experienced gun-fighters. The only question was how good were they? Sy took in a deep breath.

Frank watched for the first flicker of movement from either of them. Their eyes had narrowed, and their hands had moved even closer to their guns.

Frank knew this moment would be for ever etched in his memory – if he lived to have any memories. All the weeks of practising had inevitably led to this moment. His hand was almost touching his holster. He wasn't even aware that he was breathing. He was standing so still he might have been carved out of stone. Sy took in a deep breath.

Suddenly they went for their guns. There was a flash of movement. Surpise was stamped on their faces as Frank's gun leapt from its holster before they could even start to draw.

It was Sy who spoke first. 'Don't do anything.' Frank waited. 'Please,' he added, contritely.

'Unbuckle your gun-belts.'

They couldn't get rid of their gun-belts quickly enough. They guessed he would not kill them if they were unarmed. Their sweaty fingers struggled with their belts which finally lay on the floor.

'Now step back.'

They stepped back a few paces.

'Stop.'

They obeyed immediately.

'You've had your fun. Now I'll have mine.'

He fired, the bullet smacking into the ground an inch or so from Sy's foot. He yelped as he jumped up into the air. Frank repeated the treatment with Hank, who cursed as he too involuntarily leapt high. Frank repeated the treatment over and over again. It brought a string of curses from both of them. Hank finally stumbled and sprawled on the floor.

Frank sheathed his gun. He was aware that somebody was clapping. He had been so absorbed in his shooting that he hadn't noticed that Laurie was standing on the doorstep.

'Leave your guns there. You can get them later.' Frank had returned his attention to the two gunmen.

They shuffled away from their guns and Frank watched them until they had collected their horses and headed towards the stables.

Frank walked slowly towards Laurie. She had a welcoming smile on her face. As he drew alongside her, she opened the door wide. 'My hero,' she purred.

TWELVE

In a cottage belonging to one of Tasker's tenants, a meeting was taking place. It had been called by Bill Paterson. There were fourteen tenants present, most were standing, since there were only six kitchen chairs.

Paterson was in his early thirties. He had a friendly, open face, blue eyes and short crinkly hair. He looked the sort of person you would instinctively trust. That was why the tenants had chosen him as their leader.

'This is the first meeting we've had for some time,' he began. 'In fact, since Nathan's accident.'

'That was no accident,' said O'Shea, a belligerent Irishman.

There was a general growl of agreement.

'Well, we've all got our opinions as to what happened to Nathan. But there's no point in dwelling on it. If we rectify the wrong, if we step out from under the burden which is grinding us down – then at least Nathan's death won't have been in vain.'

There was a chorus of agreement.

'We all know that Langdon is growing. We've had the opening of the first schoolroom. The stage is already stopping twice a week instead of once. A couple of new farms have been set up on the west range, yet – we're still here, like last century serfs in England, kow-towing to our lord and master, Tasker Wesley.'

'What are we going to do about it?' demanded O'Shea.

'In the first place, it's no good just going to Tasker, and telling him we want to be paid in cash for our grain and our cattle. He'll just laugh in our faces, the same as he did to Nathan.'

'As long as he owns our land, I don't see what we can do,' said a thin, lugubrious character named Colley.

'As long as Tasker pays us in tokens, we'll never have money to spend on the things we want to spend it on. On top of that we're not getting value for money—'

'For tokens, you mean,' said a small man, named Timmins, who was the comedian among the tenants. It brought a few sniggers.

'Since we've got to go to his stores to spend it.'

'So, what can I do about it?' reiterated O'Shea.

'I don't think it's legal,' said Paterson.

'Legal or not, there's nothing we can do about it,' said Colley.

'I know some miners who are paid by tokens,' said O'Shea.

'Yes, but that's only for a few months – while they are digging the mine. Most of us have been here now for three years. We should be paid in the legal tender of the United States. Dollars.'

There was a loud chorus of agreement. It was followed by several of them asking the same question. 'What are we going to do?'

'We're going to law,' said Paterson.

This time there was a murmur of disbelief.

'What law?'

'There's no law in Langdon.'

'Tasker's the law here.'

'We haven't even got a sheriff.'

Paterson held up his hand for silence. When the muttering had abated, he said, 'I'm not talking about a sheriff, I'm talking about a lawyer.'

'Where will we find a lawyer?' demanded O'Shea. He followed it with, 'Lawyers cost money.'

'I know.' Paterson again held up his hand. 'But I've found out that there's a lawyer in Drakesville. His name is Beatty. He's willing to take on cases on a "no win, no cash" basis.'

Those assembled looked at each other while they absorbed the information. Finally O'Shea stated, 'It sounds all right. Anyhow, what have we got to lose?'

'Nothing. Because we won't have to pay anything,' said Timmins.

'If it means that someone will have to go to Drakesville to see this lawyer,' said Colley, 'you can count me out. I've got too much work to do on the farm.'

'I'm willing to go,' said Paterson. 'Only there are two conditions.'

'What are they?' demanded O'Shea.

'First that nobody tells Tasker about our plan. I don't want to end up the same way as Nathan. Is everyone agreed?'

They signified their agreement.

'Secondly, since I will probably be away for three days, I want some of you to take care of my livestock for me.'

'That's no problem,' said O'Shea. 'I'll sort it out.'

The meeting broke up shortly afterwards. The farmers wished Paterson good luck as they filed out. Some of them gave him a friendly pat on the back. Others shook his hand. He couldn't help wondering whether it was for the last time.

THIRTEEN

Although the small sitting-room was a cool room, with its solitary window facing the low evening sun, Frank felt decidedly warm. It might have been due to the close proximity of Laurie on the small settee, added to the fact that he had already drunk a couple of glasses of whiskey.

He usually drank very little. In fact he would go for months without touching a drop. However, after his brilliant display of drawing and shooting, he felt a state of exhilaration he had never known before. Not even after giving an excellent performance of one of Shakespeare's characters. Today, he really was a king, not acting one on the stage. Hadn't he proved it, when he had out-shot those gunmen? Every second of the confrontation had been stored in his mind. He knew he would examine it again and again in the days and weeks to come.

He had accepted Laurie's offer of a drink almost without thinking about it. It was, after all, only his due, that he should be fêted and fawned upon. Even the large quantity which Laurie seemed to be putting in his glass didn't worry him. Today was his day. Nothing could spoil it.

They touched glasses. He drank the burning liquor and did not show her that the unfamiliar spirit was almost choking him. It wouldn't pay for a king to display such a weakness in front of one of his subjects.

'You were fantastic. Where did you learn to shoot like that?'

'On—' He started to say "on stage". 'On my uncle's farm,' he lied.

'I've never seen anyone draw a gun so quickly. Sy and Hank are no slouches. But you had them covered before their guns had cleared their holsters.'

They were sitting close together and her hair brushed against his face. He would finish his drink, then he would be on his way.

'Tell me something.'

'What?'

'Have you ever killed a man?'

'Not yet.'

Their faces were close together. He could read the open admiration in her eyes. Her lips were invitingly close. It was funny, when they were close to his like this, he didn't notice the weak poutiness which he had observed on the first occasion they had met. He was enough of a man of the world to know that she was offering him her lips. And possibly something else besides.

To take his mind off those tantalizing lips, he drained his glass. It really was quite pleasant – after the first few mouthfuls.

'You can not only shoot, you can hold your whiskey,' she said, admiringly.

Before he realized what was happening, she was refilling his glass. Well, he would just drink this one, then he would make tracks.

Their bodies were almost touching. She was wearing a skirt and blouse and he was admiring her female shape under her blouse. He was aware that his body was responding to her closeness. More than that, he could see by the glint in her eye that she was aware of his response. He took a strong pull at the whiskey to try to restore some calmness to the situation before it got out of hand.

'My bedroom's through that door.' She pointed to a white door at the end of the sitting-room. Their faces were so close that he could feel her breath on his cheeks. A king is entitled to take a mistress, isn't he? All the kings in history had had mistresses. Why should he be so different? This one was obviously a submissive subject.

'Shall I take your boots off?'

Why not? He would feel more comfortable without his boots on. The main thing was he still had his gun.

She had taken his boots off. Kings were

supposed to be undressed, weren't they? She was leading him through the white door. Well, he'd just have a look at her bedroom before he left. It would be rude not to. The bed felt quite comfortable. He could see himself in the mirror on the dressing-table. He felt like waving to himself in the mirror. No, that would be silly.

She was undressing. Well why not? After all, it was her bedroom. She had every right to undress in it. As he had suspected, she had an excellent figure. He was admiring it, not as a prospective lover, but much as a theatrical impresario would, if he was looking for a shapely filly to include in his musical show.

It was at that moment when Sol burst into the bedroom. Laurie screamed. Sol was livid with anger. It was a case of *déjà vu*. He was holding a pistol which he was pointing straight at Frank.

FOURTEEN

Paterson decided to set out for Drakesville early. His two children were still asleep in their cots when he kissed his wife, Amy, goodbye.

She clung to him, as if unwilling to let him go. Gently he disentangled himself. He knew she was upset at the thought of him going. They had had a long and heated discussion late into the night. Finally his arguments had convinced her that if they ever wanted a better standard of living than they had, it was necessary for them to get out from under Tasker's yoke.

As he rode away from the farm he was aware that she was sobbing. It strengthened his resolve to see the business through to the end.

He passed the other tenants' farms where the corn was like a golden carpet which looked as though it could be walked on. A couple of them were already at their water butts, filling up their kettles. They waved to him as he passed.

He knew that Tasker would be on his way back

today. He would be travelling by stage, so the last thing he wanted to do would be to meet it, since it would immediately arouse Tasker's suspicions. And set him wondering why one of his tenants, who should be working in his fields, was taking time off to ride in the direction of the next town.

After he had passed Langdon, Paterson left the trail, and struck off up into the hills. He should come across the stage at about mid-day. He would be able to see it on the trail below.

As he rode along he had plenty of time to sort out his thoughts. Although yesterday, in the meeting, he had been confident that something could be done to challenge Tasker's insistence on paying them in tokens, in the light of day that confidence had soon evaporated. After all, at the end of the day, it was Tasker's land. They were his tenants. So presumably Tasker could do what he liked.

So strong was the realization that he was engaged on a fool's errand, that he almost turned his grey mare round there and then. However, he resisted the temptation. As he rode ahead, he reasoned that the tenants had nothing to lose. They had to know one way or another whether Tasker was within his rights.

Suppose Tasker had the law on his side? Then, presumably, they would have to carry on paying him exorbitant rents and crippling charges for their goods from his stores. Except that they had one choice. They could move further west.

It was something which he had thought about more and more lately. It would not be an easy decision to take. They had arrived in Langdon after a hazardous journey from the east. Although the Indian threat had more or less abated, the main danger had been from the gangs of outlaws, many of which were still roaming the country even though the Civil War had ended twenty years before. The worst threat, however, on their journey to Langdon, had been the blizzards in the winter when their wagon train had been forced to come to a halt. It had claimed the lives of both of his parents, who had been taken ill when there was no way they could get to any help. It had been a terrible time. Thankfully, he and his wife had survived and had managed to reach Langdon. The decision to move on would be an unbearably difficult one due to these events.

He was so engrossed in these thoughts that he almost missed seeing the stage-coach on the trail below. He did spot it though as it drew level with him. He was confident that no one had seen him, not even those on top.

When it was out of sight, he slowly descended to the trail. Now all he had to do was to get in touch with the lawyer, Beatty, and convince him that their cause was worth taking up. Then, some time in the future, a happier day could dawn for the tenants.

FIFTEEN

When Frank stared into the barrel of Sol's gun, he felt that his days had suddenly and irrevocably come to an end. The look of venom on Sol's face was an additional nail in his coffin. He knew he was as near death as he had been when Sol had fired at him when he was on the stage. In another flash of realization he was aware that he was now cold sober. It gave him no comfort.

'Don't kill him. Please,' entreated Laurie. She fell on her knees to plead with her brother.

Frank could see Sol's finger trembling on the trigger. His own gun was lying discarded on the floor. It was a pathetic relic of the moment when Laurie had unbuttoned his gun-belt.

Frank closed his eyes. If he was going to meet his Maker then he wouldn't want to meet Him with his last moment etched on his mind being Sol's face.

'Please let him go.' Laurie's tearful plea stung his mind. Sol's lips were set in a snarl. The finger was still trembling on the trigger. Frank's life was hanging by the thinnest of threads. Laurie had her arms round her brother's legs. 'Please,' she begged. Frank opened his eyes.

Sol was looking down at her. At that moment the realization burst on Frank like a sudden and unexpected glimpse of the sun after a thunderstorm that Sol was not going to kill him. He knew he had no logical reason for this sudden upsurge of hope. Except that he had seen something in the look that passed between Sol and Laurie.

'Get out.'

Laurie had stood up. She was now clinging to Sol's arm. Frank took a deep breath.

'Can I have my gun?'

'I said get out.'

Frank glanced at Laurie, who gave an almost imperceptible shake of her head.

Frank walked slowly out of the bedroom. He was sure that Sol wouldn't shoot him in the back. He picked up his boots from the sitting-room.

'And don't ever set foot in this house again,' were the final words Sol hurled after him.

He was glad that Hank and Sy weren't around to see him leave. If they had been, they might have been rather puzzled to see him leaving without his gun. Then it was on the cards that their puzzlement would turn to glee, when they realized the advantage they had over him. And they would hasten to turn that advantage into something concrete. No, he was glad when he had ridden out of sight of the ranch.

Well, you really made a fool of yourself, didn't you?

All right, you don't have to remind me.

Look at you, coming back with your tail between your legs. You haven't even got your gun.

I know.

It all started off so well. You managed to out-draw Sy and Hank, I'll give you that.

Thanks.

Then why did you have to go and cock everything up?

It was reaction.

Reaction, my foot. All you had to do was to say no.

I felt like a king. For the first time in my life I had faced – not one gunman, but two – you've got to give me some credit for that.

All right. But all you had to do was turn round and leave.

She was so full of admiration. She was my audience. I wanted to savour the moment to the full. That's why I went in.

Then why did you drink the whiskey? You know you can't drink.

I thought because I was king, I could do anything.

You almost ended up in bed with her.

You don't have to remind me. I'm not proud of it.

And to crown it all, you've now lost your gun.

You don't have to remind me of that either.

Mrs Tiller also noticed that Frank wasn't carrying his gun.

'You haven't got your gun?'

'No,' said Frank, shortly.

Her gaze appraised him. 'Once you start carrying a gun, you'd be better sticking to it.'

'Yeah.' Frank had poured himself a glass of lemonade from the jug she always kept in the kitchen.

'Especially with those scum of brother and sister.'

It took Frank a moment to realize that she was talking about Sol and Laurie. He finished his drink and was about to go up the stairs when her next words stopped him. 'You know what they say about them?'

'No. What?'

'I don't suppose there's any harm in telling you. Even though you are one of them.'

'Mrs Tiller, I am not one of them. I just happen to work for them. That's all.'

She gave him one of her long stares, weighing him up before replying. Finally she said, 'They're more than brother and sister.'

She was watching him to see whether he was shocked. 'Are you sure?'

'That's what folks say. Folks who've seen them together.'

He realized suddenly that that was the reason for the strange glance which had passed between them. He hadn't realized it at the time, of course, since he hadn't known about their relationship, but there had been a hidden promise in the revealing glance. Laurie had been promising Sol that if he let Frank go, then he could take his place.

It also explained why Sol should be insanely jealous of Frank's relationship with his sister. Perhaps it also explained why Laurie's husband had been killed. Maybe Sol had killed him out of jealousy. He wouldn't put it past him, having seen the undiluted hatred with which he had been regarded by Sol, before Laurie had rescued him.

Although events at the end of his visit to the Wesleys' ranch hadn't turned out as he would have hoped, Frank climbed the stairs to his room with a light step. He accepted philosophically that things could have been worse. A lot worse. One thing was for sure: in future he'd give Laurie a wide berth. He'd keep out of her way if it was humanly possible for him to do so.

SIXTEEN

Paterson's visit to Drakesville started off disastrously. The lawyer, Beatty, was not in his office. In fact he would not be available until the following day, the clerk informed him. Beatty was spending a few days in Washington and he would not be due back until the stage arrived in the afternoon.

That meant he would have to spend a further couple of days away from home. Well, there was nothing he could do about it, except wait.

Drakesville was a bustling town with wagons regularly coming and going. However, there was plenty of room for them to pass in the main street which was appropriately named Broad Street.

He stopped and asked an old-timer who was standing on a corner where he could find a cheap hotel for the night.

'Go down West Street – about a hundred yards. You'll find a hotel called Rambeau's. It's run by a Frenchman. He charges two dollars a night – one

91

dollar for the bed, and the other for the fleas.' The old-timer laughed showing gums without a single tooth between them.

Rambeau's turned out to be every bit as run-down as the old-timer had indicated. For a few seconds he was tempted to retrace his steps to where had seen a comfortable hotel. The trouble was its charges were five dollars a night. He resisted the temptation since he knew that Amy would expect him to look after his hard-earned money.

Having booked a room for the night and fed and watered his horse, he went for a leisurely stroll around the town.

He decided to visit the barber's shop. The barber, whose name, it proclaimed on the door, was Charlie Kemp, was a jovial, middle-aged man who kept up a running conversation with his customers. When it was Paterson's turn, and the lather boy had lathered his face, the barber opened his conversational gambit with, 'You're new around here?'

'Yes.'

The barber was stropping his razor lovingly. 'I thought I hadn't seen you before. Of course, I get a lot of folks in I haven't seen before – what with the town expanding the way it is.'

'I expect you do.'

'Yes, we get all kinds.' The barber stopped in the act of shavng Paterson's face, as though mentally adding up the different kinds. 'Most of them are law-abiding citizens. Some of them aren't though.' Paterson closed his eyes. 'That's it,' added the barber. 'Just relax.'

Paterson wouldn't have been relaxed if he had known about a meeting which was taking place at the Lone T ranch. Tasker had got off the stage at Langdon. He had collected his horse from the livery stable and had ridden out to the ranch. He hardly had time to shake the trail dust off when Laurie knocked at his study door.

'One of the tenants wants to see you,' she announced.

'Who is it?' asked Tasker, as he poured a glass of whiskey and lemonade.

'Colley. He says it's urgent.'

'All right. Show him in.'

Tasker was seated behind his desk when Colley came in. He stood nervously in front of him. 'Well?' demanded Tasker.

Colley's lugubrious face was creased in indecision. He gulped nervously. Finally he blurted out, 'It's Paterson.'

'What about him?'

'He's gone to Drakesville.'

Tasker frowned. 'What for?'

'He's gone to see a lawyer. His name's Beatty.'

'Go on.'

'We had a meeting with the tenants. They want

93

to get paid in cash instead of in tokens. They want to find out whether it's legal.'

Tasker banged the desk angrily. 'Of course it's legal. It's legal because it's my land. I can do what I like with it.' He was now shouting. 'If they don't like it, they can go somewhere else.'

'I – I thought you'd like to know,' stammered Colley.

'You're right. I'm grateful to you.' Tasker had calmed down as quickly as he had erupted. He rang a bell on top of the desk. After a few moments Laurie appeared. 'Colley has brought us some useful information. See that he's rewarded.'

Laurie took out a key from a drawer in the desk and went over to a safe in the corner. She opened it and took out a metal box containing a thick pile of notes of various denominations. Colley licked his lips as he stared at them.

Laurie deftly counted out ten dollars. She looked enquiringly at her father. 'Ten more,' he stated flatly. As she counted out the further money, he smiled at Colley. 'We always pay generously for information.' Laurie handed the money over.

Tasker stopped him with a warning as he headed for the door. 'We wouldn't want it to get known that you gave us the information. It wouldn't be healthy.'

The phrase stayed with Colley as he left the house. It was to haunt him for many days and months ahead.

SEVENTEEN

When Colley had gone, Laurie returned to the study.

'What was that about?' she demanded.

Tasker's face wore a thoughtful expression and for a while he did not reply. Laurie waited patiently while he was wrapped in his thoughts. Finally he sighed. 'You'd better get your brother in here,' he said.

When Sol came in he sat down on the only other chair, leaving Laurie to stand. 'Is this gonna take long? I'm in the middle of a game of quoits.'

'Your quoits can wait,' said his father, sharply.

Sol shrugged.

'Colley has just told me that Paterson is going to see a lawyer in Drakesville,' Tasker began. 'The tenants want me to get rid of the tokens system of payment.'

'Oh, they do, do they?' snarled Sol. 'Well let's go in and show them who's boss. Once and for all.'

His sister threw him a withering glance. 'Just

95

shut up and listen,' she said.

'He's going to see a lawyer named Beatty.' Tasker continued evenly. 'It could be dangerous.'

'For him or us?' smirked Sol.

'You mean because this ranch isn't rightly ours,' suggested Laurie.

'Isn't *legally* ours,' corrected Tasker. He took a cigar from a box on top of the desk, bit off the end and spat it out, then he put it in his mouth. Laurie stepped forward and struck a match and held the flame to the cigar. Tasker puffed away until it was glowing satisfactorily.

'I've never understood why the ranch isn't ours,' said Sol, sulkily.

'It's quite simple,' said Laurie, as though explaining to a young child. 'The ranch belonged to Uncle Fred. We came to stay with him. Then when Ma died he wanted to kick us out. He and Dad had an argument. Dad killed him.'

'I liked Uncle Fred,' said Sol, reflectively. 'He used to put me on his knee and tell me stories.'

'He wanted to throw us out. We had a row. It ended up in a fight and I hit him and he fell, banging his head against the fireplace. He was dead,' Tasker recited flatly.

'It wasn't your fault, Pa,' said Laurie, soothingly.

'What do you want us to do about Paterson?' demanded Sol, impatiently.

Tasker stared thoughtfully at the ash on his

cigar before replying. Then he said, 'Things are changing here. More people are coming in to the town. They've opened a new schoolroom. I suppose it's bound to happen. Things can't stay as they are. I've been in to Drakesville to see the marshal. He wants me to put forward a name to be the sheriff here. Yes, it's all changing.'

'So what are we going to do about Paterson?' This time Laurie asked the question.

'There's only one thing we can do—'

'I'll get rid of him – the same as I got rid of the other,' Sol broke in eagerly.

'You'll do nothing of the sort,' snapped his father. 'Haven't you been listening to what I've been saying? Things are changing. We've got to move with the times. Or we'll go under.'

'So you don't want the lawyer pushing his nose into our affairs,' said Laurie, thoughtfully.

'Quite right.' Her father nodded encouragingly.

'That means we'll have to give up payment by tokens.'

'Exactly.'

'But that means we'll be giving up lots of our money,' protested Sol.

Tasker waved a dismissive hand. 'We've got plenty. I've made a nice pile during the years we've been fleecing the tenants. Anyhow, I've got another ace up my sleeve.'

'So it means that you'll have to go to Drakesville, and explain to Beatty that there's no need for him to take the matter any further,' said Laurie. 'Because you've decided to do away with the token system of payment.'

Tasker beamed. 'That's it in a nutshell.'

'I don't like it,' said Sol. 'It'll mean we'll be giving in to the bastards.'

'Don't you see, we've got no choice?' Laurie explained, patiently. 'Otherwise the lawyer could find out that we don't legally own the ranch. We could get turned out, lock, stock and barrel.'

Sol scowled and stood up. 'I'm going back to my game of quoits.'

'Oh, no you're not,' said Tasker sharply. 'I haven't finished yet. I want you two to go into Drakesville.'

'What do you want me to do in Drakesville, Pa?' asked Laurie.

'I want you to see the lawyer, Beatty. Explain that I've decided to stop paying the tenants by tokens. Use your charm, get him to drop the whole matter.'

'Why can't you go?' demanded Sol.

'I've just come back from there. I've spent six hours in the stage-coach. I'm not as young as I used to be. My old bones are aching.'

'We'll go, Pa,' said Laurie, decisively.

'Good girl. I know I can rely on you. You'll go along to protect her,' he said, turning to Sol. 'It isn't safe for a young girl on the trail on her own. Not with those outlaws about.'

'It's too late to start now,' Sol stated. 'It'll be dark before we get there.'

'You'll go first thing in the morning.'

'Is that all?' demanded Sol.

'Yes, you can go. I want you to stay,' he said to Laurie.

When Sol had left the room, she sat in the chair he had vacated. She regarded her father expectantly.

'It's about putting a name forward for sheriff ...' he began.

Laurie kept a straight face, managing to conceal her thoughts. She knew that if she played her cards correctly she could get the person she wanted as sheriff. His name – Frank Lowry.

EIGHTEEN

Several times during the day Frank found himself thinking about his gun. How would he be able to get it back? It didn't take a genius to work out that if Sol had picked it up then he could say goodbye to it for good. No, his only chance of retrieving it lay in the possibility that Laurie had claimed it.

The irony didn't escape him that he was worrying about the gun at all. He had always considered himself as a man of peace, someone who stood aside from the violence and lawlessness which was rife in the West. He was a civilized person – hadn't he tried to bring some culture to the community in the form of Shakespeare's plays? Yet, here he was, feeling as keenly about the loss of his gun as if it were the most precious possession he had ever known.

He examined his conscience. Assuming he received the gun back, could he kill Sol? Unhesitatingly the answer came back as yes. Sol was one of the dregs of society who deserved to be exterminated. Sol was a killer. He had seen it in his eyes during the few seconds when Sol's finger had itched on the trigger of his revolver. The few seconds during which his life had hung on the slimmest of threads. Before Laurie had stepped in and saved him.

He was just as determined now to kill Sol as he had been when he had taken the decision in the first place. He wasn't a Hamlet-like character deciding on a course of action and then finding a thousand reasons for not carrying it out. He knew now that he could kill if the need arose. Before he had gone to the Lone T he had been beset by doubts. But, when he had outdrawn Hank and Sy, it was as if he had stepped into a new world. It had given him a feeling of power such as he had never known.

On the stage he had often felt the exhilaration and sense of power which came when he had the audience hanging on to his every word. It usually came when he was playing one of the big Shakespearean roles. He had revelled in the feeling of being in complete control over his audience. He had gloried in uttering the famous speeches of Hamlet, Lear, Macbeth or Prospero. He had thought that it had represented the pinnacle of his life. It had brought him fulfilment and the respect of his fellow-actors. But it could never compare to the moment when he had outdrawn Hank and Sy.

'Day-dreaming again?' Nat chided as he saw Frank staring into space. At that moment a customer came into the store and Frank was saved from replying.

Frank recognized the customer as Miss Chivers, the new schoolteacher. Although Nat was nearer to her, he turned and disappeared into the backroom, leaving Frank to deal with her.

She smiled at him. She was a smart young lady in her late twenties who just missed being pretty, but who had a warm smile. She was quite tall – about the same height as him, Frank noted – as they faced each other across the counter.

'How can I help you, Miss Chivers?'

'Do we have to be so formal? I know we haven't been formally introduced. But my friends call me Adele.' She extended her hand.

'My friends call me ...' he was on the point of saying Frank when he realized his mistake, 'Al,' he concluded.

They shook hands. 'What can I get you, Adele?'

She acknowledged his use of her name with a smile. 'Some flour please.'

'How much?'

'Oh, a few pounds. I'm trying to make some bread. Not with much success at the moment, I'm afraid.'

'It's in two-pound bags.'

'I'd better have a couple. It will be plenty for me to burn.'

'You're getting the oven too hot,' he explained, as he handed her the bags. 'If you put your hands in the oven, and you can count up to ten, that should be just right.'

'Knowing me, I'll end up by burning my hands.'

Frank smiled.

She seemed in no hurry to leave. 'How is the school coming along?' he enquired politely.

'It's fine. Well, that's not quite true,' she added apologetically. 'What I should have said was that on wet days it's fine. I can't get used to the idea that on fine days half of my class don't turn up.'

'It's harvest time,' Frank explained. 'Even the young ones are wanted to help on the farms.'

'I'm from back East. I haven't got used to it, yet. You're from these parts?'

'No. I'm from Chicago.'

'Not quite as far East as me. I'm from Boston.'

'You've come a long way to teach in Langdon.'

Adele's face clouded. 'There were two of us originally who intended to come out West. My husband and myself.' Frank waited for her to continue. Finally she said, 'He died last year. From the influenza epidemic.'

'I'm sorry,' said Frank, inadequately.

'Oh, I've got over it now,' she said, with a forced smile. 'No, that's not true,' she added, quietly. Her next words were spoken so quietly in fact that Frank could hardly catch them. 'I'll never get over it,' she said.

NINETEEN

Paterson had arranged to see the lawyer, Beatty, at two o'clock. He had spent a restless night; partly because of the bed-bugs and partly because of a nightmare.

In his dream he had been walking down a wide street. The sun was shining and yet strangely there was no one about. Judging by the shortness of the shadows the time was around midday. As he walked down the street he was aware of a terrible foreboding. Something was going to happen. What it was he couldn't guess. The only thing he knew was that by the time he reached the end of the street, he would know what the dreadful thing would be.

When he awoke he was sweating profusely. There was enough light from the moon to frame the window. The hotel was wrapped in silence. The bed-springs creaked protestingly as he got up and crossed to the window. He looked out at the shadows cast by the moon and shivered.

He rolled a cigarette. What did the dream mean? Did it have a meaning at all? Was it some kind of warning?

He had a cousin, Sheena, who was half Crow Indian, and who claimed to be able to interpret dreams. She maintained that 'dreamland' as she called it, and 'waking-land' were one and the same. The white man, during the centuries, had lost the knowledge how to 'read' his dreams. It was one of the prices he had to pay for his so-called civilization. What would Sheena have made of this dream he wondered.

Probably the wide street was Broad Street in Drakesville. The fact that the shadows were short meant that the time was round about midday. That would represent the time he was due to meet the lawyer, Beatty. At two o'clock.

If the dream meant anything it was that something was going to happen to him at that time. But what? Surely nothing could happen to him here. In the first place nobody except a handful of his friends knew that he was here. And they were in Langdon. In fact there was no one in Drakesville who knew that he was here. So it must all be a storm in a tea-cup, as his grandmother used to say.

Maybe he had had a bad dream because of something he had eaten. Yes, that was the most likely explanation. It was probably that cheese he had for supper. He thought it had seemed a bit rich.

He felt relieved at having discovered the probable cause of his nightmare and went back to bed. After a while he slipped into a restless sleep.

The following morning with several hours to kill he wandered idly around the town. He passed several saloons, some of which had their doors open and he was able to glimpse the men standing at the bar or playing cards. There was no temptation for him to go inside, since he was not a drinking man.

He was struck by the number of Indians who were hanging around. It was different from Langdon where you hardly saw an Indian. Perhaps as Langdon expands, he thought, it will attract more Indians. No doubt they provided a good source of casual labour. Of course they were all supposed to be living on the reservations, but that agreement, forced on the Indians after the Battle of Little Big Horn had long ago been broken. He remembered his Uncle Ted, who had been killed in the battle. He had only been a young lad but he had avidly digested any scrap of information about Custer's last stand. He remembered sitting in their living-room while the family had discussed the tragic event. He used to sit on his stool while the others sat around the fireplace.

The opinion of his parents and various aunts and uncles was that Custer was a fool. He shouldn't have ignored the advice of his scouts and led the Seventh Cavalry into battle. He should have waited for reinforcements to arrive. Especially as the cavalry were tired and weary after spending three gruelling days in the saddle. The trouble with Custer was that he had wanted all the glory for himself. And he had paid the ultimate price.

A pretty young Indian girl smiled invitingly at him as he passed. He had heard that many of them had been reduced to prostitution, but this was the first time he had seen it face to face. He shuddered as he passed by. He could not have been more shocked if he had suddenly come across a dead body on the sidewalk.

The hours passed by on leaden feet. At half past one he collected his horse from the livery stable, saddled her and led her out, after stopping to give her a drink at the trough. They would stop on the trail after leaving Drakesville and he would let her graze in the long grass. He also had a few apples in his saddle-bag. They would both enjoy eating them when he pulled off the trail. He would have plenty of time for the break; assuming he did not leave Beatty's office until three o'clock, it would still give him plenty of time to reach Langdon before sunset.

He felt relaxed as he tied the mare to the hitching rail near Beatty's office. He had forgotten all about his nightmare and was confident that once he had explained their case to Beatty, the lawyer would pursue it for them. He would soon see that it was a case of rank injustice. The upshot would be that Tasker would be forced to comply with their demands, and pay them in cash. It would mean that the standard of living of the tenants would be improved considerably. Not forgetting his own.

He smiled at the thought as he stepped on to the sidewalk and turned towards the direction of Beatty's office. He had almost reached the door when something made him turn and look down the street. The sight in front of him caused him to freeze. He realized suddenly, with a sickening foreboding, that his nightmare was about to come true.

TWENTY

The morning after Adele's visit to the store, a young lad came in. He went up to Frank and said, 'Miss Chivers sent me.'

'What does she want?' demanded Frank.

'She forgot to get some yeast.'

Frank smiled as he went to fetch it. He was about to give it to the lad when Nat spoke. 'Why don't you take it up to the school yourself?' When Frank hesitated, he added, 'You said you'd done a bit of teaching yourself. It might be interesting for you to see the school.'

Frank glanced quizzically at him. 'You're not trying to do a bit of match-making are you?'

'Who, me?' demanded Nat, as innocent as a choirboy.

'Don't deny it, you old rogue. I saw the way you disappeared when Adele came into the store yesterday.'

'So it's Adele is it?' asked Nat, with a twinkle in his eye.

Frank turned to the young lad. 'You run along. I'll bring the yeast myself.'

He glanced at Nat to see if there was any sign of triumph. But Nat kept a studied straight face. It was only after Frank had left the shop that he gave vent to his feelings.

'Yippee!' he yelled, somewhat to the astonishment of the solitary female customer in the shop.

As Frank walked up the slight hill to the school his thoughts focused on Adele. There was no doubt that she had suffered a huge tragedy when her husband had died. She had obviously been devastated by it, just as he had when Mary had been shot. Yes, they had a lot in common. Both of them had suffered from the 'slings and arrows of outrageous fortune'. Both of them had been scarred by their personal tragedies. There was one difference though: Adele seemed to have come to terms with her loss. Oh, he realized from her last remark to him that she still grieved for her lost husband. However, the fact that she had come out West on her own showed how determined she was to put it all behind her. She certainly had spirit. Behind that very feminine exterior was a very determined young lady.

While Adele had almost got over her personal tragedy, what was he doing about his? Wasn't he cosseting and nourishing it just like a new-born baby? He had to face facts: Mary was dead;

nothing he could do would bring her back to life. What if by some miracle of circumstance he managed to kill Sol? Would that bring Mary back to life? Of course not. So why not forget about this stupid idea of revenge? And start building a new life. As Adele had done.

He arrived at the school. It was a low wooden building standing proudly in its own ground. Frank felt a pang of nostalgia for the school in which he had once taught in Chicago. Perhaps even now he would still be there if only he hadn't gone to the Tivoli theatre and caught the most potent of diseases – stage lust.

The classroom was strangely quiet. At least Adele knew how to keep order, he acknowledged.

She greeted him with her warm smile when he knocked and entered the classroom. 'There was no need for you to deliver it personally, Al. Having said that I'm delighted to see you.'

There were about twenty expectant faces turned on them. Adele was wearing a white dress which accentuated her slim figure. Frank realized that he was standing close enough to her as he handed her the package, to catch the gentle fragance of her perfume. They seemed to stand in an expectant silence for ages. The moment was broken when a young voice piped up from the back of the classroom, 'Are you going to kiss him, miss?'

Adele blushed as the class burst into laughter. To hide her confusion she picked up a book which lay on her desk. 'I've just been telling them the story of one of Shakespeare's plays. It's *The Tempest*. Do you know it, Al?'

'Yes.'

She handed him the book and he flicked through it. The class had subsided after their outburst. Adele noted Frank's interest in the play. On impulse she said, 'You've got a nice speaking voice, Al. I wonder if you would do us a favour?'

'If I can.' His eyes were still fixed on the book.

'Would you read one of the speeches for us? I'm sure the class would appreciate it.'

Frank glanced up. The pupils were regarding him expectantly. He nodded thoughtfully. He flicked through the book and selected a page. He began to recite Caliban's speech.

' "Be not afeard. The isle is full of noises,
  Sounds, and sweet airs, that give delight, and
      hurt not...." '

Adele's gaze was fixed on him in rapt admiration as he delivered the speech. It did not escape her notice, however, that he was not reading it. His eyes were not following the words. He obviously knew it off by heart.

When he had finished she burst into applause. After a moment the class joined her.

'That was lovely. You should have been an actor.'

'Yeah,' said Frank.

TWENTY-ONE

When Paterson saw Sol and Laurie riding towards him he was gripped by a chilling fear. The fact that they were riding towards him was enough to make his heart sink. But the worst thing was the expression on their faces: they were both smiling at him. It was not the smile of a friendly greeting though. Their smiles were about as friendly as barbed wire.

He stood undecidedly by the door. 'Hullo, Paterson.' Laurie greeted him as they pulled up alongside.

'Going to see the lawyer?' demanded Sol.

'I don't see that it's any of your business,' said Paterson, beginning to recover from the shock.

'Oh, but it is our business,' said Laurie, as she tied her horse to the rail.

Paterson knew he should ignore them and go ahead into the lawyer's office, but curiosity got the better of him. 'What do you mean?'

'We've come to see him ourselves. On the same

business,' she stated.

They were now on either side of him, making it difficult for him to go into the office without pushing past them. 'On the same business,' said Sol, emphatically.

Paterson hesitated. He knew he could not very well go in to see the lawyer without finding out what they were talking about. 'How do you know what my business is?'

'Never mind how we know,' snarled Sol. 'We're here to stop paying the tenants with tokens.'

Paterson's first reaction was disbelief. His second was that it must be some kind of trick. 'I don't believe you.'

'Perhaps you'll believe this.' Laurie produced a letter from her bag. She handed it to him. Paterson started to read the letter.

It confirmed what they had said. Tasker stated that from now on the system of payment by tokens to the tenants would be abolished. The house-keeper and the cook had witnessed the signature. It was obviously a letter which would be considered legally binding.

Paterson's relief was still tempered with suspicion. 'It seems all right,' he stated, grudgingly.

'Each of the tenants will get one of these letters,' explained Laurie. 'As you can see, it will change everything.'

'It will change everything,' agreed Paterson

slowly, as he read the letter again. 'I've got an appointment to see the lawyer,' he added.

'There's no need to bother now,' said Laurie. 'Save your money. He charges five dollars for an interview.'

'Are you sure?'

'Positive.'

'But I've heard he takes on cases on a no win, no fee basis.'

'Oh, he does that. But he still charges five dollars for each interview.'

Sol was listening inpatiently to this exchange. 'We're wasting time,' he snapped.

'Yes,' said Laurie. She gave Paterson a long stare before moving towards her horse.

Paterson's main reaction was one of over-whelming relief as he watched them riding away. His next was that he was amazed that everything had turned out so perfectly, without him even having to see the lawyer. He had Tasker's letter in his pocket which would at last give him and the other tenants their freedom. Tenants? Huh! That was a laugh. They had been more like serfs. True Tasker had bought their grain and dairy produce, but they had never been paid in cash. But now everything was going to change. They would be able to sell their produce, get paid in cash, and save up some money. The next step would be to buy their small farm from Tasker. Then they really would be masters of their own destiny.

He could picture the faces of the other tenants when he broke the news to them. They would be as surprised as he had been. They probably wouldn't believe his news in the first place. But he had the letter to prove it, didn't he? And it had all been settled without any words being hurled in anger.

As he rode along the trail he wondered why Tasker had suddenly changed his mind. Perhaps he had made enough money and had decided that it wasn't worth bleeding the tenants dry any more. Or perhaps Tasker had seen the light and become a reformed character. He smiled at the thought. Tasker had about as much chance of changing his character as a leopard its spots.

He was whistling as he rode along. Amy would be delighted with the outcome of his visit to Drakesville. He had hardly spent any money, except for the cost of a room, a few bare essentials of food and the presents he had bought. He remembered the apples in his saddle-bag. He would wait until he had put a few more miles behind him before he stopped and shared them with his mare.

The presents he had bought for his wife and two daughters weren't much – in fact they had only come to fifty cents. It was just two lengths of ribbon. One was red, for Amy, the other was pink, for his daughters. Amy would cut it in half and give them one piece each to tie in their hair. He knew they would all be delighted with their gifts. Not only that but he was taking a few dollars of their hard-saved money back for Amy.

The evening shadows were beginning to lengthen. Like many horsemen who had been riding a particular horse for some time he often talked to the horse. 'Come on, Suzie, it won't be long now. We'll soon be home. It will be nice to sleep in our own beds tonight.' The mare, as if she knew what he was saying, pricked up her ears and seemed to lengthen her stride. He was concentrating so much on his own horse that he did not hear the sound of the horse which was following. He did however hear the sharp 'crack' of a rifle. But by then it was too late.

TWENTY-TWO

Paterson's body was discovered the following day by the stage-coach driver. He first spotted a riderless grey horse wandering around ahead. He slowed the stage-coach in order not to frighten it, scanning the trail ahead for any sign of the rider who might have fallen from the horse.

He eventually spotted the figure of a man by the side of the trail, stopped the coach and dismounted. Several startled faces peered at him from inside the coach as he examined the body. 'He's dead,' he confirmed.

Although the driver did not recognize the dead man, one of the two passengers who had approached the body, did. He was a stocky character named Stan Bowles, brother of one of Tasker's tenants. 'It's Bill Paterson,' he said. 'I'd know him anywhere.'

'Where does he live?' demanded the driver.

'Langdon. He's one of Tasker's tenants.'

The other passenger, a thin man with spectacles, named Hewlett said, 'He's been shot in the back.'

'Probably by a gang of outlaws,' said the coach driver. 'I've heard there's a gang hanging around these parts.'

One of the women who had been in the coach, whose name was Mrs Parr, approached the body. She gasped when she saw the blood covering his back. 'Is he dead?' she asked.

'I'm afraid so, ma'am,' said the driver.

'We can't leave him lying here,' she stated.

'He lives in Langdon, about six miles ahead. I'm not taking him on the stage,' announced the driver.

'I'm riding up on top,' said Bowles. 'He can travel up there with me. That is if the ladies don't object.'

'I don't,' said Mrs Parr.

'No,' said the driver positively. 'There'd be blood all over the place. It would take ages to scrub it off.'

The impasse was solved by Bowles who said. 'There's the spare horse behind the coach. We could put Paterson on to his horse and I'll ride the spare horse into Langdon.'

'Yes, I suppose we could do that,' confirmed the driver.

'He's obviously been murdered,' said Hewlett. 'Shouldn't we look for clues?'

'He's been killed and robbed,' said Bowles.

'Whoever did it wouldn't have left any clues behind.'

'We're assuming he's been robbed,' said Hewlett, stubbornly. 'Perhaps he's been killed for some other reason.'

'It will be easy to check whether he has been robbed,' Mrs Parr pointed out.

'Don't look at me,' said the driver. 'It was your idea.' He turned to Hewlett. 'You search him.'

'All right.' Hewlett first put his hand in the saddle-bag. The others watched as he searched. When he withdrew his hand it was empty. 'There's nothing there,' he announced. Gingerly he put his hand in one of Paterson's trouser pockets. 'Nothing,' he again announced. The body was lying on its side and he was forced to roll it over to get at the other pocket. When he withdrew his hand he pulled out a couple of lengths of ribbon. 'That's all that's in there,' he stated.

'We'd better get him on his horse,' said the driver. 'I've been hanging around here long enough.'

Amy had not been particularly worried when her husband had not returned the previous night. She had reasoned that it might have taken a couple of days before he was able to see the lawyer. After all, Beatty would be a busy man. And it wouldn't be expected that Bill could see him straight away. So, she decided to put any doubts behind her and just wait until her husband returned.

She had put the children to bed and was about to shut the hen-house for the night when she had the first inkling that something was wrong. A rider was approaching the farm leading her husband's grey mare. When he drew closer she could see that what she had mistaken for a blanket over the saddle-bag was really a figure. Her heart lurched. She knew with a sickening certainty that her whole world had suddenly come to an end.

TWENTY-THREE

The impressions of his visit to the school stayed with Frank for some considerable time. They were pleasant thoughts, not like those of revenge and death which he had lately been harbouring. He had seen young children with the thirst for knowledge which all young children have until it is so often blunted and finally dampened by events, or worse, by ignorant adults.

He had enjoyed reading from *The Tempest*. For a few moments he had recaptured the magic of being on the stage, of holding the audience in the palm of his hand, of seeing the admiration on Adele's face. Yes, he had definitely enjoyed his visit to the school.

Shortly after his reading, Adele had dismissed the class. She had told him that they were all itching to get back to their farms. She had come up with the compromise of teaching them in the morning, and letting them go home in the afternoon, while the harvesting season lasted.

He had watched as they left the classroom in an orderly file. Once outside, however, they had whooped and laughed as they were leaving the school.

'There's nothing like the laughter of young children,' Adele announced.

'No, I don't suppose there is,' agreed Frank.

She had brought some lunch with her, far more than she would want. Would he like to share it with her? After a moment's hesitation, he agreed. 'I didn't bake the bread, so it's fine to eat,' she informed him, with a smile.

They ate their food on the veranda. Afterwards they sat in companionable silence for a while, then they started talking about books. 'It's the one thing I'm short of,' she explained. 'I wasn't able to bring many with me when I came here.'

'I've got quite a few packed away in my trunk,' said Frank. 'Although I don't know whether they'll be suitable for young children.

'You never know. Anyhow I might be able to use them the same way I used *The Tempest*, by just picking out the story for the children.'

'I'll go through them and see what I've got,' Frank promised. 'There is one I know I've got which might save you some work. It's Lamb's *Tales from Shakespeare*.'

She smiled her thanks. 'I'd appreciate that.'

They talked about authors they liked, and found they had a lot in common. They both liked the popular English author Charles Dickens and Adele promised to lend Frank a couple of titles which he hadn't read. It was during a lull in the conversation that Adele said, 'How is it that an educated person like yourself is working as an assistant in a store here in Langdon?'

As soon as she said it, she regretted it. She saw the change in his face. It was as if a mask had suddenly fallen over it. 'That's my business,' he said sharply. Shortly afterwards he left.

It was the following morning when the news spread throughout the small township that Bill Paterson had been killed. 'The stage-coach driver found the body as he was coming in yesterday evening,' Nat told Frank.

'He was murdered?'

'Oh, yes. Shot in the back. Mrs Parr said there was blood all over the place.'

'Bill Paterson? He's one of Tasker's tenants. He's been in here a few times.'

'That's right.'

'Who'd want to kill him? Could it have been outlaws?'

'Maybe. And there again, maybe not.'

'All right you old weasel, what else is there?'

Nat grinned. 'He'd been to Drakesville, to see the lawyer, Beatty. He was representing the tenants to try to get Tasker to release them from payment by tokens.'

'Had he now?' said Frank, thoughtfully.

'I'm not saying there's any connection,' said Nat, blandly.

'But there could be,' supplied Frank.

Nat shrugged. 'Your guess is as good as mine.'

'I suppose Tasker could have had him killed to stop him seeing the lawyer,' said Frank, slowly.

'I wouldn't go around saying things like that,' said Nat, warningly. 'Not if you want to live to a ripe old age.'

'Wait a minute. Didn't you say that he was killed on his way back to Langdon?'

'That right.'

'So presumably he saw the lawyer. What point would there be in killing him afterwards? No, I suppose it has to be outlaws,' he concluded, regretfully.

'It's getting that it's not safe to go out,' said Nat. 'At least not without a gun.'

The statement reminded Frank that his own gun was still over at Tasker's ranch.

TWENTY-FOUR

Frank had been half-hoping Adele would come into the store during the afternoon. He knew she finished at the school at midday and thought that maybe she would come in to see him. He had unlocked his trunk the night before and rummaged through the books. He had found a few which might be suitable for young children such as *The Swiss Family Robinson*, *The Coral Island*, and *Robinson Crusoe*. He had brought them with him wrapped up in a parcel. Nat had eyed the parcel on several occasions. Frank had ignored him, knowing that he was getting more and more curious.

Finally Nat could control his curiosity no longer. 'I see you've got a parcel.'

'Yeah.'

Nat rubbed his hands together. 'Something important?'

'You could say that.'

'It looks like something pretty heavy.'

'Oh, so-so.'

'Well are you going to tell me, or aren't you?' Nat finally blurted out.

'Oh, you mean the parcel,' said Frank, feigning innocence. Nat scowled. 'I suppose I might as well tell you, or you'll burst your braces. They're books.'

'Books?'

'For Adele. For the school.'

'Ah!' exclaimed Nat, with sudden enlightenment. 'So you two got on well together yesterday?'

Frank's face clouded. 'More or less.'

'She's a nice young lady.'

'You don't have to tell me that,' said Frank sharply.

'She's the sort of lady who anyone would be pleased to be walking out with,' persisted Nat.

'Oh, why don't you mind your own business, you interfering old warthog,' retorted Frank. But Nat was pleased to note that there was more banter in his tone than displeasure.

In fact it was late in the afternoon when Adele finally came in. She was wearing a pale-yellow dress. Nat regarded her admiringly as she walked towards the counter. 'May I say how you've brightened an old man's afternoon, Miss Chivers,' he said.

'Well, thank you for the compliment. But I expect you say that to all your lady customers,' she said with a smile, as she looked around in vain for Frank.

'If you're looking for Al, he's in the back room,' said Nat. 'You can go through.'

She went inside where Frank was busy weighing out seed. He looked up as she entered. They stared at each other for what seemed like an eternity, each trying to read the other's thoughts. Finally she said, 'I was wondering whether you had found any books.'

He wiped his hands on his apron and took it off. 'I've found a few.' He produced the parcel.

'Thanks,' she accepted it.

An embarrassing silence developed between them. For two people who had so much to say to each other yesterday it grated on Frank. He reasoned that he was the one to blame. 'About yesterday ...' he began.

'I shouldn't have said it,' she countered quickly.

'It was my fault.'

'I had no right to pry. It was just that....'

'Yes.'

'Well we seemed to be getting on so well together. It just slipped out.'

'One day I promise I'll tell you what you want to know.'

She sighed. 'I'll keep you to that,' she said, with a smile.

Frank knew it was absurd. But the one thing he wanted more than anything else in the world at that moment was to take Adele in his arms and kiss her. They were standing close together. Was he wrong, or was there a hint of expectancy in her eyes? He wondered what her reaction would be if he did try to kiss her. Her sweet lips were invitingly close. When the young lad had shouted yesterday 'Are you going to kiss him, miss?' she had blushed. Was that because she had the same thoughts in his mind as he had now? The only way to find out was to take her in his arms. He was just about to when a cutting voice came from the doorway. 'I was told you were in here.' It was Laurie.

Adele stepped back hurriedly. The movement was not lost on Laurie whose lip curled in a sneer.

'Can I get you something?' asked Frank evenly.

'Daddy wants to see you. Now,' she hissed.

Frank glanced apologetically at Adele. 'I'm afraid I've got to go.'

'I understand. Thanks for the books,' she added as she passed Laurie without giving her a glance.

'I'll get my horse,' said Frank. 'It's round the back.'

They rode in silence. Laurie's face was like thunder as she repeatedly flicked her horse with her crop. Finally she snarled, 'So you fancy the plain schoolteacher, do you?'

'She's not plain,' Frank retorted hotly.

He realized immediately that she had trapped him. The strength of his denial had betrayed him. A triumphant sneer spread on her face,.

'Well you can forget about her. Do I make myself clear?'

He knew this was not the time or place to argue with her. His first priority was to find out what Tasker wanted. He racked his brains but could not come up with an answer.

When they reached the ranch, Laurie led the way into Tasker's study. He was seated at his desk and glanced up as they entered. 'Sit down,' he said to Frank.

Frank sat. He was uncomfortably aware of Laurie who was standing just behind him. Tasker was gazing at Frank thoughtfully. Finally he said, 'Laurie tells me you can handle a gun.'

The statement took Frank by surprise. His mind rapidly flicked through reasons for Tasker's observation but he couldn't find one. 'I think I can look after myself,' he stated cautiously.

'Good. That's what I like to hear,' Tasker beamed.

'I told Daddy how you outdrew Sy and Hank,' supplied Laurie.

'Well perhaps they're not the two fastest gunmen—' Frank began.

'But you took on the two of them. That shows courage,' interrupted Tasker.

Frank waited for him to come to the point. He was aware that Laurie had moved closer to his chair. He couldn't help feeling that he was the fly and Laurie was the spider, and that when she was ready she would pounce.

'I've brought you here to offer you a job,' said

Tasker.

'A job?'

'The town is expanding: we've opened a new school; things are changing around here; new people are moving in. There's one thing a growing town like this must have. Law and order. That means a sheriff.'

It began to dawn on Frank the purpose of his visit. He was already one of Tasker's employees and what better way could Tasker have of keeping control over the town than by appointing him as sheriff? Especially since Tasker had found out that he could handle a gun.

'... So I'm offering you the post,' Tasker concluded.

'He'll take it,' said Laurie positively.

Frank felt that the spider had finally struck.

TWENTY-FIVE

His initial reaction to refuse had been tempered by the thought that perhaps it might turn out to his advantage after all. Not so much financial advantage, although Tasker had pointed out that he would be getting three times as much as sheriff as he was getting as an assistant storekeeper. No, perhaps here was his chance to get even with Sol once and for all. As sheriff he would have the law on his side. He could put Sol behind bars for the murder of his wife, Mary. And probably for the murder of Laurie's husband. And also probably for the murder of Nathan Tiller. Yes, he would have the opportunity of putting Sol away for a long time. Probably for the rest of his life. These thoughts passed through his mind as he waited for Laurie to bring the coffee Tasker had asked her to get for them.

'Laurie likes you,' Tasker stated.

'She's – she's a very attractive woman,' admitted Frank.

'Not only that, but she's got a good head on her shoulders,' said Tasker, proudly.

At that moment Laurie had returned with the coffee. 'Well, have you made up your mind?' she demanded, as she handed Frank his cup.

'Give him a bit more time to think about it,' remonstrated her father. 'It's bound to have been a surprise.'

When she had handed her father his coffee, Laurie perched on the corner of his desk. She smiled at Frank as she swung her leg idly. He could not help glancing at her very shapely leg. The spider hasn't finished with me yet, he thought. To try to take his mind off Laurie he asked Tasker. 'How would I go about being appointed as sheriff? Would I have to have some of the local people recommend me?'

Laurie choked on her coffee. Tasker smiled benignly. 'No. If I recommend you, that's it. I've seen the marshal at Drakesville. He'll accept whoever I recommend.'

'But wouldn't I have to be sworn in?' he asked, deliberately avoiding looking at Laurie.

'I'd give you a letter to take to the marshal telling him that you're the person I've selected. He'd swear you in and give you your star. You'd come back here, I'd fix up an office for you, and then of course we'd have to build a gaol. I'd provide the money. There'd be no problem.'

He said that he wanted a bit more time to think

it over. 'I'll make sure he accepts,' Laurie told her father.

They went now in the small sitting-room outside Laurie's bedroom. He was sitting on the settee and Laurie was sitting near him. 'I want you to take the job,' she began. 'I know you can do it. It will give you status in the town. It will make me proud of you.' Her eyes shone as she leaned towards him.

'It's – a difficult decision,' said Frank, lamely.

'It's quite easy.' She had moved closer to him so that now their bodies were touching. 'All you have to do is to say yes.' There was a huskiness in her voice which hadn't been there before.

'What about Sol? He hates me.'

'That's one of the reasons I want you to take the job.'

'I don't understand.'

'You don't know what it's like living under the same roof as him. He – he makes me do things. Dirty things. I'm frightened of him. He's mad. I want to see him put behind bars for the rest of his life,' she concluded vehemently.

Her outburst surprised him. He realized that, for the first time since they had come into the house, she wasn't putting on an act. This was the real Laurie, a Laurie who was in deadly fear of her brother.

Perhaps this was a golden opportunity to find out more about Sol. 'Tell me more about him.'

'Only if you promise to take the post of sheriff,' she replied, craftily.

He was cornered. But he had the feeling that this was going to be his chance to start getting even. As Shakespeare had put it, 'There is a tide in the affairs of men, which taken at the flood leads on to fortune.' Well he had better make sure he took advantage of the tide. 'I'll take it,' he said.

'Oh, Al, I'm so pleased.' Her delight was genuine. She kissed him lightly on the mouth.

'Tell me more about Sol,' he said.

'He has murdered – several people.'

Frank's interest quickened. 'You mean Nathan Tiller? And your husband?' he probed.

'Oh, they're all in the past,' she dismissed them with a wave of her hand. 'You'll never be able to make them stick. I'm talking about something more recent.'

'How recent?' Frank realized that his throat had become dry. This might be the lead he would want to pin a murder on Sol.

'Oh, a few days ago.' She had recovered her composure. Now she was playing games again. She was fingering his hair and twining a curl around her finger.

He knew it was essential for him to get more information. 'As recent as that.'

'Can't you guess who?' She was nibbling at his ear.

'Well it wouldn't be anybody in Langdon.'

'It wasn't far outside,' she retorted, with triumph in her voice.

It hit him with the force of a full hundredweight sack. The person she was talking about was Bill Paterson. But surely she and Sol were in Drakesville when Paterson was killed? That's what local gossip said. So how could Sol have been involved in the murder?

He put the question to her. She was now lightly brushing her lips against his. 'I'll tell you one day. Soon,' she promised.

'Why not now?' He kissed her lightly. If this was the way he was going to get the information, then so be it.

She drew away. 'When you've got your star pinned on your chest.' There was a wealth of promise in her eyes. Frank knew that she was not just talking about Paterson's murder. He also realized that she was not going to take any chances. There was no doubt that she would give him the information he sought. But on her terms. And in her own time.

He stood up. 'I'd better go.'

'You'll be going to Drakesville tomorrow?'

'Yeah.'

'It's a day's ride. You won't be back until the next day. You come straight here. No matter how late it is. I want to see that badge on you. Promise.' She walked her fingers over his chest.

'I promise.'

He turned and was about to go out through the door when she stopped him. 'Haven't you forgotten something?'

'Have I?'

She disappeared into her bedroom. When she came back she was carrying a gun. His gun.

He took it from her. 'Thanks.'

'Haven't you forgotten something else?'

She kissed him. It was a kiss which implied that it was merely a preliminary for other things to come.

TWENTY-SIX

Frank rode slowly back to Langdon. He was aware of the gun in his saddle-bag. It was the gun with which he hoped to bring Sol to justice. He told himself he was not interested in being a sheriff for any length of time. He would take the post just in order to see that Sol was put away for life. There was no doubt that he was a murderer. Hadn't Laurie confirmed it? And so he deserved to be punished. And he, Frank Lowry, would be happy to do it.

He was busy with his thoughts and hadn't noticed which direction he was taking when he arrived in Langdon. When he looked up he realized he was nearing a small group of three cottages. Although he hadn't called there before, he knew that Adele's was the middle one.

On impulse he dismounted and tied up his horse. He pushed open the wooden gate. Adele answered his knock and her initial surprise was quickly followed by a welcoming smile. It dimmed when she saw the serious expression on his face. 'You'd better come in,' she said, holding the door open for him.

When they were seated facing each other in the small living-room, she said, 'Would you like something to drink?' He shook his head.

They sat in silence. They were both tense. Adele was rubbing her hands together nervously. 'I've got something to tell you—' Frank began.

'If it's something about your past, perhaps it would be better if I didn't know,' Adele blurted out.

'What do you mean?' he was puzzled.

'If you've been in some sort of trouble, it doesn't matter. It wouldn't alter the way I feel about you.' She had gone pale.

'It's nothing like that. Oh, I admit I've got a secret. But it's not a guilty secret. I haven't broken the law.'

'Are you sure?'

'Of course I'm sure. This is what happened—'

He started to recount the series of events beginning with the actors coming to Langdon, then Mary being shot by Sol. 'Oh, how horrible!' she exclaimed. He then explained how he had hoped one day to be revenged on Sol. And that now the chance had come, he was going to accept the post of sheriff in order to put Sol behind bars for good.

He waited for her response. He knew that it was

vitally important for her to understand. And to condone what he intended doing.

'Revenge is a terrible thing, Frank,' she began finally. 'It eats away at the person like maggots inside an apple. It changes the person's whole life. It clouds his judgement.'

'Are you saying I'm wrong to want revenge?' he demanded, sharply.

'All I'm saying is that in the beginning you were justified in the way you felt. But that was some time ago. Time is a great healer. I know, it's almost cured my own personal tragedy.' She drew in a deep breath. 'Time will dim your desire for revenge. Believe me.'

'Are you saying I shouldn't go ahead and become sheriff?'

'To be a sheriff you've got to have a gun. And know how to handle it.'

'If that's what you're worried about, I can assure you I've got a gun. And I've learnt how to use it,' he said, harshly.

She stared at him as though seeing a new aspect to his character she hadn't discovered before. 'I still don't think you should go through with it,' she said finally.

'I'm sorry, Adele, but I've made up my mind,' he said, stubbornly. 'I'm going into Drakesville tomorrow to be sworn in as sheriff. I'll be back the following day. I was hoping you'd understand and support me in my venture.'

'It's her, isn't it?' said Adele vehemently. 'She's got some sort of influence on you.' She noticed his hesitation. 'I've heard about her reputation. They say she's man mad. And what she can't get from other men she gets from her brother.'

Frank stood up. 'Goodbye, Adele,' he said formally.

'I'm sorry. I shouldn't have said that.' Frank had already opened the door. 'Don't let's part like this.' She watched him as he walked away. Her eyes followed him as he mounted his horse. 'God be with you, Frank,' she whispered, as he rode away.

TWENTY-SEVEN

The following morning Frank started off early for Drakesville. His anger that Adele had not supported him had evaporated. He had made a mistake in going to see her. He did not know what he had expected. She could never understand the depths of despair to which he had been plunged when his beloved Mary had been shot in his arms. Of course he acknowledged that Adele had had her own personal tragedy. But she hadn't been involved in it, in the same sense that he had been involved in his.

He went over for the thousandth time the scene in the hall where they had been playing *King Lear*. They were nearing the end of the last scene when Sol and his companions had suddenly appeared in the hall. Sol had started shooting. He had continued with the play, determined not to let a drunken lout close it down. The others in the cast had left the stage but he had carried on. He should have left with them, but no, he wanted to prove that he was not afraid of a drunken lout. He wanted to prove that 'he' was in control, not the drunkard with the gun. So he had stayed on the stage. And Mary had been shot.

He had told himself a thousand times since the event that he should have left the stage with the others. Then Mary would still be alive. But no, he was determined to prove something to himself. And so Mary was dead. And he had to carry the cross of being responsible for her death. That's why Adele would never understand the depth of the hatred he felt for Sol. She couldn't be expected to.

Although he had started off early, Mrs Tiller had been up, baking some bread. The mouth-watering smell hung around the kitchen. When he entered she had looked up from kneading the dough.

'I'm going to Drakesville. I'll be away for a couple of days,' he informed her.

'Expecting trouble?' she asked drily, glancing at his gun.

'Protection,' he responded.

'I'll get some food for you to take.'

'There's no need to bother.'

She had brushed aside his refusal. 'It's a six-hour ride. You'll get hungry on the way.'

When he arrived in Drakesville he made straight for the marshal's office, having first asked directions from an old-timer outside a saloon who was as gnarled as the stick he was trying to whittle. He found the office without any problem and tied up his horse.

He went into an outer office where a clerk was seated at a high desk. The clerk, who had been peering at a document, looked up. 'Yes?' he asked, brusquely.

'I'd like to see the marshal.' He handed the clerk Tasker's letter of introduction.

The clerk read it. His demeanour immediately became more deferential. 'I'll see if the marshal can see you. I won't be a moment.' He disappeared into an inner room. When he returned he said, 'Marshal Smythe will see you.'

Frank stepped inside the inner room. The marshal was seated behind his desk. Behind him was a photograph of himself in his army uniform with a major's insignia on his epaulette. 'Sit down,' he said with a welcoming smile, as though offering a seat to his favourite lieutenant.

Frank sat. The marshal went into a speech in which he described the responsibilities of becoming a sheriff. Frank nodded at suitable intervals. The marshal then explained that since Al had been recommended by Tasker Wesley, he was obviously a suitable candidate for the post and concluded by saying that if Al was prepared to accept the position of sheriff then he would swear him in.

He was sworn in and left the office shortly afterwards wearing his star of office on his chest.

He was officially the Sheriff of Langdon.

His next priority was to find somewhere to stay the night. He passed a couple of cheap boarding-houses before finally arriving at the Majestic Hotel. He decided he might as well treat himself to a good room for the night, after all, he was a sheriff, so he had a reputation to uphold. He smiled at the thought.

He booked in and ordered a meal. While he was eating he found his thoughts turning to Bill Paterson. A couple of nights before he had also booked into a hotel. It probably wouldn't bave been this one, since Paterson had a wife and family to support. No, it would probably have been one of the cheaper boarding-houses. Then afterwards he had gone to see the lawyer, Beatty. On his way home he had been ambushed before he had been able to reach Langdon. Local opinion was that he had probably been shot by the gang of outlaws who were known to be in the locality. It was the same gang who had held up the train just outside Drakesville and got away with some gold bullion a couple of weeks before. Well that was one thing he wouldn't have to worry about as sheriff of Langdon, since there wasn't a station there.

However Laurie had hinted that Sol had been involved in Paterson's death. But how could he, since, according to local gossip, he and Laurie had both spent the night in Drakesville?

Or had they? Perhaps the gossips were wrong. Perhaps they had ridden back the same day as Paterson. Then, when they had caught him up, Sol had shot him. But why? It probably had something to do with Paterson seeing the lawyer about the tenants wanting to be paid in cash. And maybe it had a lot to do with the fact, as Laurie had stated, that her brother was mad.

Sol and Laurie would have stayed in this hotel if they had stayed the night, since it was the best hotel in Drakesville. There was one way to find out whether they had stayed here. When he had finished his meal, he approached the desk clerk.

'What can I do for you, Sheriff?' There was a deference in his tone due to Frank's status.

'I'm trying to find out if Sol and Laurie Wesley stayed here two nights ago.'

'Just a moment.'

The clerk glanced through the hotel register. He finally looked up. 'Miss Laurie Wesley stayed here. But she was on her own.'

So Sol hadn't stayed in the hotel. Which was the story they had spread around. Instead he had lain in wait for Paterson. And then shot him.

I've got you, Sol Wesley, he thought, exultantly.

TWENTY-EIGHT

His mood would have been less buoyant if he had known what had taken place in Laurie's bedroom at about the same time.

Laurie was sitting at her dressing-table, pinning up her hair when Sol burst in. His face was livid with anger. 'Is it true?' he snarled.

'Is what true?' She had gone pale.

'That skunk who's working in our store is going to be the sheriff of the town?'

'Why don't you ask Daddy?'

'I'm asking you.' He swung her off her stool. Holding her with one hand he slapped her hard with the other.

'Don't hurt me. Please,' she whimpered.

'The truth.' He spat out. 'If you don't tell me....' He raised his hand again, threateningly.

'Yes, it's true.' She tried to pull away from him, but he held her firmly. 'Daddy went to see the marshal when he was in Drakesville. He had to put someone's name forward.'

'Why didn't he ask me? Why didn't he put my name forward?'

'I don't know. Let me go.' She struggled, but he still held her tightly.

'I know.' He thrust his face close to hers. 'You put his name forward, didn't you? You scheming bitch.'

He hit her again, releasing her at the same time so that she sprawled on the floor.

She was sobbing as he stood over her. 'You fancy that skunk, don't you? You think that with him as sheriff, you will be able to get your own back on me. But your little plan won't work. Because I've seen through it.'

She had crawled away from him and now stood up. 'What are you going to do?' she cried in panic.

'He'll be coming back from Drakesville tomorrow, with his star on his chest. But it won't be there long, before they'll be burying him with it.'

'No!' she screamed.

'Oh, yes,' he smirked. 'So you say goodbye to him. Because you won't see him again. And just in case you're thinking of warning him, forget it. You'll stay on the ranch until I say you can leave. Someone will be watching to see that you do. This is just a reminder of what will happen to you if you don't do as I tell you.' He hit her full in the stomach. She doubled up with pain.

He laughed as she lay on the floor, retching. He watched her for a few moments. Finally he said,

'See you later, Sis.'

Frank was riding leisurely towards Langdon. He was only a few miles out of the town and in less than an hour he would be in his lodgings. Then he planned to have a bath and afterwards call on Adele.

The harsh words which had been spoken on both sides had been troubling him while he had been away. He had found a shop in Drakesville and bought her a present. It was a book which he knew she would like. It was one of the novels by her favourite author, *Emma* by Jane Austen.

He rounded a bend. Three men were standing in a line barring his way, Hank, Sy and Sol. The three had guns in their hands.

'Get down,' commanded Sol.

He knew he stood no chance. If he tried to spur his horse to ride between them, they would easily gun him down. If he tried to draw his gun while still in the saddle, he would be shot full of holes before his gun could clear its holster. He knew he had to get down from his horse.

He turned his horse so that he was partly shielded by the animal. He knew he would have to go for his gun as soon as he touched the ground. Sol was the middle of the three. He was determined that, since he was going to die, he would take Sol with him. The incongruous thought struck him that Adele would never get her book now.

'Hurry up,' snapped Sol.

He glanced at their faces. If he was looking for compassion, he was unlucky. They were all killers. And here they were in their element. Because the odds were stacked so high on their side that they knew they could not lose.

He would go for Sol first. Then, if he had a second chance, he would go for Hank. Hank was to Sol's right and it would be the easiest second shot – assuming he had a chance of a second shot. For a man who was about to die, he was surprised how calm he felt.

He swung slowly down from the horse, his left hand holding the reins. He had positioned the horse between Sy and himself. He drew as he was getting down and got a shot off at Sol before he sprawled on the floor. The suddenness of the movement took them by surprise, since they were expecting a target which was on its feet. Now he presented a more awkward target to aim at.

He had missed Sol with his first shot but felt a thrill of satisfaction as his second bullet caught Sol in the chest. Bullets peppered the ground around him and he felt a tug of pain as one caught his leg. However, he took careful aim to make sure of killing Hank. His bullet caught him in the forehead and blew out his brains.

His joy was short-lived. A freak shot from Sy hit his Colt and sent it spinning out of his hand and before he could get to his knees to recover it, Sy was standing over him, his gun poised.

Any fleeting thoughts that Frank harboured about Sy giving up the battle now that the other two were dead were dispelled by his words.

'You've done me a favour, Sheriff. With Sol out of the way I'll be able to put my plan into action. I aim to marry Laurie. Then all the Wesley ranch will be mine.'

Frank watched his finger tighten on the trigger. There was the sound of an explosion. But it wasn't Sy's gun because Sy was now sprawled in the dust, obviously dead.

Frank stared up at his benefactor, who was now approaching with his gun in his hand. It was the man with spectacles who had come in on the stage. 'Are you all right?' he asked, with concern.

'Yes. Thanks to you,' said Frank, getting up, gingerly.

'I'm sorry I couldn't get a shot in earlier. But your horse was in the way.'

'I'm just glad you came when you did, Mr—?'

'Hewlett. I work for the Pinkerton Agency. I've been investigating the bullion robbery near Drakesville. I thought the person who was killed here a couple of days ago might have been shot by the band of outlaws.'

'You're on the wrong trail,' said Frank. 'His name was Paterson. He was killed by that madman,' he said, pointing to Sol.

'Ah, well, I'll just have to keep on looking,' said Hewlett. 'Perhaps I could give you my address, Sheriff. Then if you get any information about them you could pass it on to me.'

'I'd like to help,' said Frank. 'But I'm afraid I won't be around. Well, not as a sheriff. I only took the post to right a wrong.'

'Seems as good a reason as any,' said Hewlett, as they rode together towards Langdon.

Adele flew into his arms as he knocked the door of her cottage. 'Thank God, you're safe,' she said, as she clung to him tightly as though determined he would never go away again.

'It's all over,' he said.

It was several years later when she confided to the eldest of their three children that they were the sweetest words she had ever heard.

L